SAVING CASEY

KAREN MUELLER COOMBS grew up outside a small town in Northern Alberta, where there was plenty of room for her dogs, her cats, and her horse. At bedtime, some of these furry friends would often snuggle down with her, and together they would listen to the haunting symphony presented nightly by croaking frogs and howling coyotes.

Today, Karen lives with her husband Jon, her son Cameron, and her daughter Carlin in Carlsbad, California, where, to her joy, frogs croak outside her windows and the cries of the coyotes echo through the dark canyons. She still misses Sabrina, her last dog, a Bouvier des Flandres, who always tried to "snuggle in" during nighttime thunderstorms, and who died in 1990. Since Sabrina's death, Karen has struggled to resist the urge to adopt every animal she sees at the pound.

SAVING CASEY

KAREN MUELLER COOMBS

AN AVON  CAMELOT BOOK

SAVING CASEY is an original publication of Avon Books. This work has never before appeared in book form.

AVON BOOKS
A division of
The Hearst Corporation
1350 Avenue of the Americas
New York, New York 10019

Copyright © 1992 by Karen Mueller Coombs
Published by arrangement with the author
Library of Congress Catalog Card Number: 92-90337
ISBN: 0-380-76634-5
RL: 4.3

First Avon Camelot Printing: December 1992

CAMELOT TRADEMARK REG. U.S. PAT. OFF. AND IN OTHER COUNTRIES, MARCA REGISTRADA, HECHO EN U.S.A.

Printed in the U.S.A.

OPM   10   9   8   7   6   5   4   3   2   1

To my mother,
Catherine Jean Parsons,
for her unwavering support and constant encouragement
through the years.
With love and gratitude.

Chapter One

"**W**hat ya doin'?"

Scott jumped back, scared it might be Dr. Wilder. But it was only Jackson, his assistant.

"I was just petting him."

"Don't. They're research animals, not pets. Making pets of them might louse up the test results."

Scott went back to his job—feeding and watering the rats and mice at the Institute for Better Living. I.B.L. for short. There were a zillion of the critters, and it would take him nearly an hour to make his rounds.

Jackson watched as Scott poured pellets into a feeder. "How old are you anyway?" he asked.

"Twelve."

Jackson shook his head. "Twelve." He said it as though being twelve should be illegal, then added, "But what can I expect? No adult will do this work for what we pay. So, just do your job and don't handle the goodies. I don't want some snot nose wrecking test results."

"What are you testing?" Scott asked, curious about why some animals had a bandaged patch on their

1

bodies. It was only his second day of work and he hadn't learned not to ask too many questions.

"Right now we're testing a new ingredient for lipstick," Jackson explained. "The company that hired us wants to know if the chemical will hurt human skin. So we smear it on the test subjects and watch what happens."

"What could happen?"

Jackson shrugged. "Nothing—we hope. If something is toxic, the skin might get sore or the subject might eventually get tumors. Then we assume it's not safe for people."

"What happens to the animals that get tumors?"

Jackson grinned. "Well, we have this roomful of cats in the back of the building. If a mouse gets a tumor, we feed it to the cats. And then we watch the cats to see if they get tumors from eating the mice." His shoulders jogged in a silent laugh.

Scott sucked in his breath, loud enough for Jackson to hear.

"Just kiddin'," Jackson said then, and Scott breathed again.

"So, what does happen to them?"

"They die."

Scott's insides flip-flopped. Until he'd heard about the job at the lab, he didn't even know animals were used in research. Then he'd figured they were just used for blood samples or maze tests. Things that didn't affect them much. He never thought they died.

Scott decided not to ask what kind of research the lab was doing on the dogs, the dogs on the other side of the gray door marked Authorized Personnel Only. Suddenly he was glad he wasn't authorized. He didn't want to know what was happening on the other side.

The thought of dogs like Casey growing tumors made his insides squirm.

Dogs. Scott had always wanted a dog. But dog dander made his dad sneeze his guts out, made his eyes run and his nose stuff up, so all Scott could do was dream about the day he would be old enough to have a place of his own, a dog of his own. In the meantime, he walked dogs. The job at the lab was only for the rest of the summer. He'd been walking dogs for four years.

Casey was his favorite. There was something about the way Casey carried himself, about the way he laid his head on Scott's knee and looked at him with his brown eyes that made Scott's insides feel like warm honey was flowing through him. Scott sometimes forgot the golden-colored mutt wasn't his own, sometimes expected, when he woke, to hear Casey's tail smack a "good morning" on the bedroom floor.

Dogs. The dogs had almost made him quit the job the first day. The barking and howling coming from the other side of that door was what did it. Like the yowling at a boarding kennel or the dog pound. But at least at those places you knew the dogs were just ticked off or lonely. Who knew why the dogs at the lab howled? Scott didn't. And now he didn't want to.

Jackson sauntered back to his office cubicle, took a slug out of his giant-sized bottle of Coca-Cola, then belched. Scott couldn't figure out how Jackson could drink so much Coke. He had a bottle on the go all the time. Jackson was a Coke addict, Scott decided, chuckling at his little pun.

Scott finished his work, but before he washed up, then signed the chart that showed what time the animals were fed, he sneaked back and gave the mouse he called Joe a tickle. Too bad about Jackson's test results.

Outside, Scott took a lungful of fresh air before climbing on his bike. At least today he hadn't minded the smell so much. Yesterday it was almost as bad as the barking. Like a hospital. Only mixed with animal smells too. Pungent and musty at the same time. Definitely not what you'd call sweet.

The barking assaulted Scott's ears until he reached the driveway at the far end of I.B.L.'s parking lot.

I'll give Casey and the others an extra good run this afternoon, he decided, thinking of the lab dogs behind the gray door.

Chapter Two

"How was work today?" Mrs. Richmond asked when Scott got home. His mother was a teacher's aide and was home for the summer.

"I found out what they're doing to the mice and rats," Scott told her. He didn't mention the dogs. If she thought the new job upset him, she might make him quit, and he needed the money to buy a computer.

He told her about the skin test. Mom shook her head. "I know a lot of sick people have been saved because of medical research done with animals, but I didn't know my lipstick was tested on animals first."

"Me neither," Scott said. "I guess I'll learn a lot about stuff like that working at the lab.

"I'm going to walk the dogs," he said then.

"All at the same time or in separate batches?" Mrs. Richmond asked.

"Separate batches," Scott answered. "Astrid's in heat so I can only walk her with Petunia."

"Are you sure you should be taking her out at all? Is it safe?"

"Yeah, it's fine. Astrid's a Great Dane, remember.

5

Even if other dogs hang around, they're not going to bother her much."

"Okay," Mom said, brushing her bangs out of her eyes. Mrs. Richmond had short hair combed back from her forehead. Only her hair didn't want to go back, so she was always brushing at it and threatening to get it shaved off. "Astrid and Petunia, eh?" she said then. "A Great Dane and a Pekinese. The thought of those two together always gives me a laugh." She went off, chuckling, then called back over her shoulder, "Oh, I almost forgot. The reason I asked is because if you're going to walk them separately you'll only have time for one batch before dinner. Your father has bowling tonight, so we're eating early."

"Okay. I'll save Casey and Boover for later."

"Oh, Scott." His mother was looking at him with a hopeful arch in her eyebrows. "Would you take Julie with you? She's bored and driving me bananas."

"Aw, Mom, do I have to? She can't make it one block anymore without asking to be carried. She's such a pain."

"If that's your attitude, don't bother," Mrs. Richmond snapped. "I certainly wouldn't ask you to do anything you don't want to do."

Scott heaved a sigh. "Oh, all right. It's just that the job takes twice as long when she tags along." Snatching a cookie, Scott went off to find his four-year-old sister.

As far as Scott was concerned, his first eight years of life had been perfect. He'd had his mother and father to himself. There had been no one making a mess of his things, no one bugging him to make mucky cakes in the sandbox, no one whining to get her own way and throwing tantrums when she didn't. He'd liked being an only child. Then Julie was born. . . .

Julie was sitting in the sandbox stirring a bucket of soggy sand with one of Dad's screwdrivers. "Hi, Hot Scott," she said, squinting up at him standing against the sun.

"Hi, Cool Jule," Scott muttered, grudgingly giving one of her long, blond ponytails a tug.

Julie stopped stirring long enough to carefully bend the fingers of one hand into the "I love you" sign that she had learned from *Sesame Street.*

Scott ignored it. "I'm going to walk Petunia and Astrid. Want to come?"

"Yay!" Julie squealed, jumping up and tugging at her brother with gritty hands. "Let's go.

"I'm going with Scott," she shouted at her mother as they headed for the door. "I get to hold Petunia's leash!" She squished up her face and gave Scott a mushy smile, the way she always did when she wanted her own way. "Don't I?"

Later, after they'd eaten dinner and Mr. Richmond had left to go bowling, Scott phoned Tim, his best friend. Dr. Wilder, who operated the lab, was Tim's uncle, though you'd never know it to look at them. Tim and his younger brother had both been born in Korea and adopted by the Wilders as babies, so, except for all of them having dark hair, none of the Wilders looked alike.

"Hey, Muttman," Tim said, using his favorite nickname for Scott. "Haven't seen you since this morning. What's up?"

"Want to help me walk Casey and Boover?" Scott

liked having company on his walks, especially in the evening.

"Just a sec. Mom!" Scott heard Tim shout. "Can I walk the dogs with Scott?" After some mumbling, Tim came back on the line. "Sorry, I've got to help Mom hang some wallpaper. Would you believe some blue and pink stuff with birds on it? Who-o-o-o-o-pee!"

"Oh," Scott said sympathetically, "sounds like a *lot* of fun. Don't glue yourself to the wall." A picture flashed into Scott's head of Tim writhing behind a sheet of pink peacocks spread-tailed among blue leaves. "On second thought," he added, "glue yourself behind the wallpaper. Then I can bring tour groups through your house and charge them admission to see the only living, breathing wallpaper in the world. I'll have my computer in no time."

"Go walk your dogs." Tim laughed and hung up the phone.

Scott stopped at the Jeffersons' house first, to pick up Boover, a shaggy, black Bouvier des Flandres.

Boover yelped like a puppy and wriggled all over when he saw Scott with the leash, even though he was long past middle age. "Settle down," Scott ordered. "You might step on my foot." Having Boover step on his foot was almost as bad as having Astrid step on it, since Boover weighed over a hundred pounds.

The dog stood still while Scott clipped on his leash, then pranced obediently at Scott's side as they headed toward Casey's house.

When he neared Mrs. Sanchez's small, white house with the green trim, where Casey lived, Scott noticed that the gate to the backyard was open. Since Casey never wandered, he didn't worry about it.

As he neared the fence, Scott whistled the special two-note whistle he used for Casey, but the dog didn't respond. "Hey, Casey," he called, "want to go for a walk?" That would get him moving.

When Casey still didn't come, Scott shrugged. The dog was probably in the house with Mrs. Sanchez, although she usually left him outside until after Scott walked him.

Scott knocked on the tattered screen door, wondering if Mrs. Sanchez was ever going to get her doorbell fixed.

The shuffle of the old woman's footsteps sounded slower than ever to Scott as Mrs. Sanchez came to the door.

"You've come for Casey," she said, a waver in her voice.

"Yes," said Scott. "Is he ready?"

Mrs. Sanchez shook her head. "Come in for a minute, Scott." Scott looped Boover's leash over a knob on the rusty iron porch railing, then followed Mrs. Sanchez down the hall to the kitchen. In the four years he had been walking her dog, Mrs. Sanchez had never invited Scott inside before. What was going on?

She's going to fire me, he thought. Or maybe Casey's dead. Both thoughts made Scott's stomach churn, because either way he wouldn't get to see Casey.

Mrs. Sanchez pulled out a chair and pointed to it with a prune-wrinkled hand.

Scott sat, holding his breath.

Her head jerking slightly, like a yellow canary pecking at a string of millet seed hung in her cage,

9

Mrs. Sanchez perched herself on the edge of a chair across from him. Scott noticed that her eyes were brimming with tears.

"Casey's gone," she said, twisting a hanky between her gnarled hands.

"He's run away?" asked Scott. He started to get up. "I can find him. I know I can. I'll start looking right now. We can post notices, put an ad in the paper."

Mrs. Sanchez shook her head. "He didn't run away. I sent him to . . . the pound."

For a minute her words didn't register in Scott's brain. He stared at the old woman, his eyes narrowed. "The pound?" he asked then. "The pound? Why?"

"I didn't know what else to do." Mrs. Sanchez's voice wavered, and she dabbed at her eyes with the twisted hanky. "I'm seventy-eight years old. I haven't been well. I can hardly look after myself and the house, much less a dog. And . . . and it's getting so there's not enough money for dog food, and then, too, there's your fee to walk him."

As if the shock of her words had sharpened his senses, Scott noticed for the first time how shabby Mrs. Sanchez looked, as though she needed someone to pick her up and brush her off, to tidy the white hair that was straggling in narrow ribbons around her face and neck, to wrap a bright, new shawl around her shoulders. It was the first time he had ever seen her with a hair out of place. Then he saw the unwashed dishes in the sink, the dust balls in the corners, the grimy floor, the crumbs on the table. And he noticed the smell. Partly dog smell, but something else too. Perhaps a mixture of old-people smell and unscrubbed bathrooms and unemptied garbage. Then he remembered her words and forgot everything else.

"But I would have walked him for free!" he cried. "And why the pound? We could have found him a home somewhere in the neighborhood. I know we could have."

"I know how you feel about him," Mrs. Sanchez explained. "You love him as much as I do. But I knew you'd want him for yourself, even though you couldn't have him. You'd just end up miserable, since there was no way he could be yours. So I thought it would be best for all of us if I sent him to the county pound and let them find him a home."

"But he's not a puppy," Scott said. "People who go to the pound want puppies."

"He's a lovely dog. They told me they would try very hard to find him a good home. They promised. I *made* them promise."

"But the pound," moaned Scott.

"He'll be fine," said Mrs. Sanchez, dabbing again at her eyes. "He'll be fine." But Scott couldn't tell if she was trying to convince him or herself. Perhaps she really believed Casey would find a good home. Perhaps she didn't know. . . .

Thirty days. That's all the time Casey had—providing he stayed healthy and adoptable. Thirty days. Then if no one wanted him, he would be killed and that would be the end of him.

Scott choked back the sob that had crept silently into his throat.

Chapter Three

Scott ran until his lungs ached and his throat felt on fire, hoping to escape the picture of Casey he carried in his head—a picture of Casey, his nose pressed against a wire cage, waiting for Scott to come and take him for his walk.

He had started running as soon as he slammed out of Mrs. Sanchez's door, almost forgetting to unhook Boover and take him along. The dog had loped happily alongside him for a time, but now started nudging Scott with his body, as if some long ago memory told the dog Scott needed directing, like the cows Boover's ancestors had herded and protected in the distant past.

Finally Scott became aware of what Boover was doing and he slowed to a walk, the dog panting beside him. "Sorry, Boover," Scott said. "I forgot how hot you get in this weather." He brushed the dog's heavy eyebrows back and looked into Boover's gentle brown eyes. "Good dog."

Boover wagged his hind end and butted his head against Scott's thigh. "I know," Scott sighed, his voice breaking. "You're wondering where Casey is.

Well, you don't want to know." He swallowed a gulp of tears. "And I'd like to forget."

But Scott couldn't forget. He had to get Casey out of the pound, and he had to do it soon, before some stranger got him.

"Heel, Boover," he said. "I'm taking you home."

"So what are we going to do about Casey?" Tim asked a short while later. He had talked his mother into giving him a break when Scott showed up. Now, he wriggled his nose, pushed his glasses up, and squinted at Scott.

Usually Tim cursed when his glasses slid down. "Aw, bull feathers," he would mutter. "I'm going to get contacts. This nose will not hold up a pair of glasses."

"But Emily McNulty likes your glasses—and your nose," Scott would tease.

"That's because Emily McNulty wears glasses, too, and because Emily McNulty has a banana nose," Tim would reply. "Emily McNulty would like Gonzo's nose for heck's sake."

Today, though, there was no complaining and no teasing.

"We've got to get Casey out of the pound," said Scott. "And we have to do it soon, because if we don't, they'll kill him."

"Maybe he'll get adopted," suggested Tim. "He was lucky once before. Maybe he'll be lucky again."

"You mean because four years ago he wandered into Mrs. Sanchez's yard and she kept him? I guess that was lucky. But he was a cute puppy then. He's not a cute puppy anymore. That's what people adopt. They don't adopt full-grown mutts even if they are

13

gentle, and smart, and—" His voice cracked and he was silent.

"So, I repeat, what are we going to do?" asked Tim.

"Tomorrow morning, first thing, we're going to go to the pound and get him. We'll tell them Mrs. Sanchez changed her mind or something."

"But where will we take him? You can't take him home. And I can't bring him here." Tim's younger brother, Brad, had been bitten by a dog when he was three and had a screaming fit whenever one came near him. "There's no way I could even bring him into the yard," Tim explained.

"I know. I know. I'll figure something out—even if I have to stay up all night to do it. Just be at my house by eight tomorrow morning, okay?"

Tim raised his fist in a thumbs-up signal. "Eight o'clock," he agreed. "And stop worrying. You'll come up with something."

When he got home, Scott went in search of his mother. He found her in the bathroom, washing Julie's hair. As usual, Julie was squealing like a tortured pig.

"Mom, I need to talk to you," he said loudly, slouching against the doorjamb.

"I can't hear a thing," Mrs. Richmond shouted. "Wait until I'm finished." She took the hand shower and started squirting Julie's hair. "Maybe next time I'll use cold water and really give you something to scream about," she told Julie in an exasperated voice. "And how did you get that awful bruise on your leg? Roughhousing with Scott, no doubt."

Scott backed out of the room. In his bedroom, he

flung himself on the bed and buried his head under a pillow, drowning out Julie's squeals. How could he think of a plan if it wasn't quiet enough to think?

A while later his mother knocked, then stuck her head in the door. "What are you trying to do, smother yourself?" she asked.

"I'm thinking about it," Scott mumbled from under the pillow.

"Anything I can do?"

"Push on the pillow real hard," suggested Scott.

"That's not what I meant," said his mother, perching herself on the edge of his bed.

"I know." Scott sat up.

His mother looked at him, her lips puckered. "It's something serious, isn't it?"

Scott nodded.

"Okay, let's have it. Between us we should be able to find a solution."

"I hope so," said Scott. "'Cuz if we don't, Casey is *gone.*"

Scott told his mother what had happened, encouraged by her whispered "Oh, no!" and "That's terrible."

When he finished, he looked at his mother expectantly, hoping for an immediate answer to his dilemma. "Poor Mrs. Sanchez," sighed Mrs. Richmond. "I had no idea she was in such dire straits."

Scott's jaw dropped. "Poor Mrs. Sanchez?!" he asked in amazement. Apparently his mother hadn't gotten the point at all. "You mean poor Casey. Unless he's adopted, it's Casey who's going to be killed, not Mrs. Sanchez."

"I know," said his mother. "But it sounds as though Mrs. Sanchez needs someone to adopt her, too."

15

Scott thought about that for a minute, remembering how shabby the old woman had looked, how messy and run-down the house was getting. "I suppose you're right," he agreed. "But first I have to think about Casey. Thirty days sounds like a lot, but it really isn't much time, Mom. What can I do?"

Mrs. Richmond pushed her hair back off her forehead and tugged at her blouse, soaked as usual from Julie's bath-time antics. "I don't know, Scott. I wish you could bring him here, but you know that's impossible."

"What if he never came in the house?"

His mother shook her head. "Your father's miserable enough just from being around you after you've walked the dogs. I don't think the backyard is a solution."

At that moment, Julie called. "Mommy! Mommy! Come here. I'm cold. I want to get out—right now." Scott's mother pushed herself off the bed and sighed. "We'll just have to do some more thinking—after Julie's in bed," she said, then added with a shake of her head, "That girl sure does enjoy her sleep lately." She was on her way out the door when she turned and asked, "Have you thought about a boarding kennel?" before she disappeared down the hall.

A boarding kennel. Of course, Scott told himself. Some place Casey could stay until Scott found him a new family in the neighborhood. But boarding kennels cost money. And he'd have to pay for it. Scott didn't think his dad would agree to foot the bill.

His computer money. If he wanted to save Casey, he'd have to spend his computer money. But he'd been working so hard for that money, he thought, then shook his head. Forget the computer, he decided. He could get a computer anytime. There'd never be another Casey.

A few minutes later he was dialing the number of the nearest kennel.

When Scott hung up the phone he did some figuring. He had enough money to buy Casey six days at a kennel. Not much time. He shook his head. What he needed was some place cheaper. Cheaper as in free. Then he could really take his time finding Casey the right place to live. He'd just have to do some more thinking.

By the time Scott's father came home from bowling, Scott had a plan worked out. He hoped his father would agree to go along with it.

"Hi, Pops," said Scott after his father had settled himself in his recliner with the evening paper.

His father's eyes, the same blue-green as Scott's, peered at him over the top of the sports section. "Hi, good buddy."

"How'd you bowl? Did you win?" Scott asked. He wasn't very interested at the moment, but thought it might be wise to get the conversation going before he hit his father with the Big Question.

"Nope." Mr. Richmond lowered the paper. "They whipped our butts. But we're getting better." Mr. Richmond wasn't a very good bowler. He and his friends spent most of the time throwing gutter balls and telling rude jokes. Scott figured they went bowling mostly for the laughs, not for the game itself. But his father had won the trophy for the most improved player last year, so who could say?

Mr. Richmond buried himself behind the paper again.

"Uh, Dad," Scott said, "could I talk to you for a

minute?" He shoved his hands deep into his jeans pockets to keep them still. Whenever Scott was nervous he cracked his knuckles. It drove his father crazy.

Down came the paper. Mr. Richmond's bushy blond eyebrows lowered. "So, talk."

Scott took a deep breath, then told his father what had happened to Casey. "You see," he finished, "unless I get him out of the pound, he'll probably be killed. But there's nowhere for him to go."

"And you can't bring him here because of my allergies." Mr. Richmond sighed. "Oh, boy. I've felt rotten about you not being able to have a dog before because of me, but now I feel *real* rotten."

Good, thought Scott. Guilt. That's exactly what he wanted his father to feel. It would make him more willing to listen to Scott's suggestion.

"He might get adopted, you know," Mr. Richmond said then.

Scott nodded. "Yeah. I guess that would be better than him getting killed. But I don't think his chances are very good, him being older—and a mutt. And even if he did get adopted, I still . . . wouldn't . . . see him anymore," Scott finished quietly.

Mr. Richmond nodded. "True."

"I thought about buying him some time in a kennel," Scott said then, "but that costs a lot of money and I can only afford six days." He put that bit in to make sure his father knew he was willing to pay for the kennel himself. More points on his side, Scott was certain. "But then, I came up with another plan. It'll save Casey's life and it's a lot cheaper than a kennel."

Mr. Richmond's eyebrows zoomed up his forehead. "Okay, let's have it."

"What if—" Scott had to stop for another deep

breath. "What if we get Casey out of the pound and take him back to Mrs. Sanchez's? Only she won't be responsible for him. I will. I'll go over every day and feed him, clean up the yard, brush him, and walk him. I'll buy the dog food and anything else he needs."

Mr. Richmond's eyebrows dropped again.

"Just until I find him a good home in the neighborhood," Scott added quickly, his fingers crossed inside his pockets, because he had no intention of looking for a new home for Casey. He would simply tell his father he couldn't find one. Then, when Mr. Richmond saw how well the new arrangement was working out, Casey could be his dog forever. Only he'd live with Mrs. Sanchez, not with Scott. The only difficulty Scott could think of was that Mrs. Sanchez was old. If anything happened to her, he'd have to come up with a new plan. But he'd think about that when he had to.

"Hmmm-mm-m."

Scott couldn't tell if Mr. Richmond's *hmmm-mm-m* was a good sign or a bad sign. "Dad?" Scott peered at his father, hoping to see the answer he hoped for written in his eyes.

Mr. Richmond grinned. "Go for it," he said and held out his hand, palm up.

Scott yelped with glee as he gave his father five. "Thanks, Dad," he said. "I'll rescue Casey first thing tomorrow."

"Hold on," said Mr. Richmond. "What did Mrs. Sanchez say about your idea?"

"I thought I'd better ask you first," Scott explained.

"Good thinking. But you make sure you check it out with her before you go charging down to the

19

pound and end up with a dog who has nowhere to go."

Scott nodded.

"And since you're not the original owner," his father continued, "you'll probably have to adopt him. Otherwise you'd have to ask Mrs. Sanchez to go down there, and it might be too hard on the old lady. So, tell you what. I'll give you a letter saying you have my permission to adopt Casey. And here. You'll need this." He reached into his pocket and pulled out his wallet, then handed Scott some money. "This should cover the adoption."

"Gee, thanks, Dad," said Scott, feeling a burning tingle start behind his eyes and at the back of his nose.

"And, Scott," said his father as he once again raised the paper. "Don't worry about spending your own money on Casey's food. Your mother and I'll take care of that."

Scott left the room as quickly as he could. He knew if he so much as gave his father a thank-you hug, he'd start blubbering.

Chapter Four

By morning, Scott's blankets were corkscrewed from all his tossing and turning. As he stumbled downstairs for breakfast, he noticed Julie, still sound asleep in her room across the hall.

"Is that sister of yours awake yet?" Mrs. Richmond asked as Scott entered the kitchen.

"She's still out of it," Scott answered, knuckling his sleep wrinkles. He opened the cupboard to pick a cereal, then closed it again and grabbed a banana. No appetite. How could he feel like eating when Casey was at the pound wondering when Scott was coming to take him for his walk?

"I read somewhere that children only grow while they're asleep," said Mrs. Richmond, interrupting his worrying. "If that's the case, I swear Julie is going to end up ten feet tall." She sighed and poured herself a cup of coffee, then looked at Scott.

"Pull up your pajama leg," she ordered around a mouthful of muffin.

"Huh?"

"Pull up your pajama leg. I want to see if you've got any of those bites Julie has on her legs. She looks

21

like she's been attacked by a swarm of fleas. Those dogs of yours haven't been sending little gifts home with you, have they?"

Scott shook his head, then pulled up his pajama leg. Here he was, all worried about Casey, and his mother was inspecting him for flea bites. Next to Casey, a few flea bites didn't seem very important.

"See. Nothing," he said, jerking his pajama leg down.

"That doesn't prove Julie's bites aren't from fleas," said his mother. "Fleas often pick one family member to feast on and leave the rest alone. I guess Julie just tastes better."

"Good." Scott stuffed the banana into his mouth so his mother wouldn't expect him to talk anymore. Today, he didn't even want to listen, much less talk. That didn't stop his mother though.

"You haven't noticed Julie playing rougher than usual, have you?" she asked then.

When Scott shook his head, she continued. "I just can't figure out why she's getting all those nasty bruises." She rested her chin on one hand and smiled a crooked smile at her son. "If I didn't know better, I'd swear you'd been using her for a battering ram."

Sometimes I'm tempted to, Scott thought. "Gotta go," he said then, when he saw Tim skid his bike to a stop outside.

"Oh, that's right," said his mother. "You're going to rescue Casey from the pound." She got up and came around the table to Scott. "Here's a kiss for good luck," she said, planting her lips on his cheek.

"Thanks, Mom," Scott said. "I just hope we don't need it." Perhaps Casey was already adopted, he thought. Or . . . He tried to shove the next thought into a dark corner of his mind, but out it popped again. Or . . . maybe Casey was already dead. He'd heard about the pound making mistakes like that, about people coming to claim their lost dog the day after it got picked up, only to learn it had already been killed. *So sorry. A regrettable mistake. Nothing, of course, we can do to correct it.*

"You say his name is Casey?" the attendant asked, after Scott and Tim arrived at the animal shelter.

Scott nodded. "He belonged to Mrs. Sanchez at 421 Bolero Drive. He came in yesterday morning."

The attendant punched some keys on her computer.

Pins and needles. I was on pins and needles the entire time. Scott had heard that expression many times, but until that moment he'd never known what it meant. Now, waiting for the attendant to find the information on Casey, he understood.

Pins and needles. Whoever made up that expression was dead on, Scott thought, dead on. Dead, he groaned silently. That word is not allowed, he scolded himself. *Not* allowed.

At least one thing had gone okay that morning. When he had told Mrs. Sanchez his plan, she had started patting the back of his hand. "Oh, Scott," she had said, her eyes sparkling with tears, "what a wonderful idea. Why didn't I think of it?" She had gone immediately to the garbage can outside the backdoor and retrieved Casey's food and water dishes.

"He's about the size of a Dalmatian," Scott told the attendant, who was still punching keys. "Only he's a mutt. Sort of honey-gold with some black spots on his nose and chest. His ears are floppy."

"I remember him," said the attendant. She was a

23

young woman with long, black hair tied back in a ponytail. If it hadn't been for her uniform, she would have looked like one of the teachers at school. "He was a relinquish," she added.

"A relinquish?"

"That's what we call an animal whose owner had to give it up. As opposed to one lost or abandoned."

"Oh," said Scott. The pins and needles stabbed him deeper as the woman kept up her search for Casey's information. "Can't we just go out there and have a look?" he asked, thinking he could find the dog faster than she could find the file.

"Got it," she said then. She studied the computer screen for a minute. "Ah-ha," she said as she read. And, "Um-m-m."

"So, what cage is he in?" Scott asked, impatient it was taking so long. "Just tell me, okay?" He knew he was being rude, but he didn't care. All he cared about was Casey.

The woman's next words slammed the breath right out of him. "He's gone."

"Gone? Gone?" Scott's voice rose to a squeak. "He can't be gone. He only came in yesterday. So he can't be gone. He better *not* be gone." Scott stood for a moment, stunned.

Then, "You already killed him, didn't you?" he accused quietly, his eyes narrowed.

The woman shook her head. "Someone took him," she explained. "Late yesterday afternoon—after I went home."

"He was adopted?" Scott's gloom lifted a bit, but then settled again. Adopted or dead, it made no difference. Either way, Casey was gone. Unless . . .

"Who adopted him?" he asked. "Where do they live?"

The woman shook her head. "I can't tell you that."

"Why not?"

"Can you imagine what would happen if we gave out addresses and all the people who changed their minds about giving up their pets started harassing the new owners to give them back?"

"But just this once?"

Again a shake of the head.

"Then the phone number. So I can call and make sure they like him and really want to keep him? You could even call for me."

The woman hesitated and Scott thought there might be hope. Then she shook her head again.

Tim tugged at his arm. "Come on, Scott," he urged. "Give it up."

Scott resisted, tempted for a second to leap over the chest-high counter and read Casey's file himself, to dash out the door and charge up and down the rows of cages, just to make certain Casey wasn't in one. But he only nodded and followed the blurring, yellow tee shirt of his friend out the door to his bike, the sound of the caged dogs, barking out their confusion, their anger, and their sorrow, ringing in his ears.

Chapter Five

"**S**o, what now?" Tim asked. The boys were slouched on Scott's front step.

Scott sniffed and rubbed an arm across his eyes, then his nose. "I guess I'll have to go and tell Mrs. Sanchez what happened. That'll be fun. She was so excited about getting Casey back."

"Want me to go with you?"

"Naw. It might get real embarrassing if she cries or something."

"There's nothing wrong with crying, you know," Tim scolded. "In fact, my uncle said there's a chemical in sad tears that isn't found in other tears, like onion tears. They think crying when you're sad must be good for you."

"Yeah, sure," muttered Scott. "As long as no one sees you doing it."

"Don't sweat what other people think," said Tim, pushing himself off the step and heading toward his bike. "If it bugs 'em, they can go . . . go . . . pee up a rope. See ya later." But before he rode off, he pushed his glasses up his nose and added, "I'm really sorry about Casey."

"I know," said Scott. "Thanks."

After Tim disappeared, Scott went into the house. He found a note from his mother saying she had taken Julie to the library and clothes shopping and would be home around four. He washed his face and blew his nose. Then he laid the money and the letter his father had given him on the tray where Dad put his loose change and his wallet when he came home.

He took his time eating lunch. That way he could go right from Mrs. Sanchez's to the lab. And work would be a good excuse to get away if the old woman started ranting.

At Mrs. Sanchez's, the door was flung open while he was raising his hand to knock. Only it wasn't Mrs. Sanchez on the other side. A girl about his own age stood there staring at him, her unblinking brown eyes surrounded by the longest, thickest eyelashes Scott had ever seen. Her dark hair was pulled up on either side of her head into two ponytails held by elastics with gigantic pink plastic crayons attached. She would have been real cute, Scott thought, except that her nose looked sort of squished.

Then she spoke. "You must be the dog boy."

For a moment, her rudeness made Scott forget all about Casey. "My—name—is—Scott," he said slowly, as though to someone who couldn't understand English well. "Who are you?"

"Oh, Scott," said Mrs. Sanchez coming up behind the girl, "you're here at last. And you've met Cristina. She's my great-niece, come to spend the summer with me and give me a hand around the house. She just arrived this morning. What a surprise. I didn't know she was coming." The old woman

27

raised herself on tiptoes and peered over Scott's shoulder. "Where's Casey?"

Scott sucked in a lungful of air, worried about how Mrs. Sanchez would take the bad news. "He's already been adopted," Scott mumbled, as though afraid saying the words aloud would finally make it true.

"Pardon?" asked Mrs. Sanchez.

The girl, Cristina, turned and said something in Spanish to her great-aunt. Scott heard Mrs. Sanchez gasp softly. Then she leaned her head against the doorjamb. "Gone," she said. "Gone for good."

Scott nodded, reluctant to trust his voice.

Mrs. Sanchez straightened and pushed a few loose strands of hair into place. "Well, it was worth a try," she said. "I'm sorry it didn't work out. Thank you, Scott. Now, come in for a snack. Cristina has already made some delicious *sopaipillas*. Have you ever had a *sopaipilla?*"

Scott shook his head. "A soap—soap—?"

Cristina giggled. Mrs. Sanchez smiled. "A *sopaipilla,*" she said. Then, more slowly, "Soap-eye-pee-ya."

Sopaipillas, it turned out, were deep-fried pastries, sprinkled with powdered sugar and dipped in honey. They were, Scott decided, delicious. The only thing that would make the moment better was the sound of Casey's tail thumping on the floor beside him. He wondered whose floor Casey's tail was thumping on now.

As he sat there licking his fingers, Scott noticed that already Mrs. Sanchez's kitchen floor looked cleaner, even though Cristina had been there only a short time. The house smelled fresher too. He was glad the girl had come to stay. That way, Mrs.

28

Sanchez wouldn't miss Casey so much. How long would it be before *he* stopped missing him?

"Where you from?" Scott asked Cristina when his fingers were clean and he had tongued his teeth enough to be certain he had no chunks of pastry stuck to them. Mrs. Sanchez was outside, putting Casey's dishes back into the garbage, and the silence seemed worse than the risk of saying something dumb.

"Calexico," She replied at last.

"Where's that?"

"Brother! Don't you know anything?" Cristina shook her head and her ponytails swished across her face, a few hairs sticking to some honey that clung to her lips. She pulled the hairs free and said, "It's only about one hundred and twenty miles from here. Near the border—by Mexicali, Mexico."

"You're from Mexico?"

Cristina rolled her eyes back into her forehead and gave an exasperated sigh. "I said *near* the border, not *across* the border. Calexico is in California, just like Carleton."

Scott felt his face flush. "Sorry," he said. "I'm not too great in geography." He had a lot more questions, but was now too intimidated to ask. He needn't have worried.

"Next I suppose you'll want to know how old I am," Cristina said unexpectedly.

"Sure," said Scott. "I'm better at numbers than I am geography."

His attempt at a joke was rewarded with a grin from Cristina. "I'm twelve," she said. "And just to save you the trouble, my last name is Martinez. I'm five feet tall. I'm going into the seventh grade. I have two older brothers, one older sister, one younger sis-

29

ter, and a baby brother. Mrs. Sanchez is my mother's aunt. I call her *tia,* which is Spanish for 'aunt.' Anything else you want to know?"

Scott's face felt hot enough to fry the *sopaipillas.* There was a lot more he wanted to know, but he doubted he could think of a thing to ask while his head was boiling. He was glad Mrs. Sanchez chose that moment to come into the kitchen.

"I'm so glad you two are getting to know all about each other," she said.

"Well, he's getting to know all about me," Cristina said. "But except for seeing he has blue eyes, a blond rooster-tail cowlick, and a zillion freckles, I know diddly about him. You can fill me in later," she added, grinning at her great-aunt.

Scott wished he could crawl under the table and dissolve.

"Now you've gone and embarrassed him," Mrs. Sanchez scolded Cristina. She smiled at Scott. "You can tell Cristina has decided to become one of those T.V. reporters who uncovers crime and injustice."

"An investigative reporter," Cristina interrupted.

"Anyway," Mrs. Sanchez continued, "she loves to snoop. But I'm afraid she's in for a boring summer if all she gets to do is pump me for gossip and help out around the house. I was hoping she'd meet some young people her own age and get to do something exciting, but no one will even talk to her if she keeps on being such a tease." The old woman shook her head affectionately at her niece. "If you can stand her, maybe the two of you can go swimming once in a while," she suggested, "or maybe when you walk Casey—" Mrs. Sanchez's hand came up and covered her mouth. "I keep forgetting," she said quietly. Then, as though echoing Scott's thoughts, she added, "I keep hearing his toenails clicking across the floor and his tail smacking against the linoleum."

They were silent, as though listening for Casey's nail clicks and tail smacks.

"I suppose that will go away after a while," said Mrs. Sanchez.

Scott nodded, but secretly, he doubted he'd ever stop listening for Casey or watching for him to come lolloping around a corner. "I've got to get going," he said. "I have to be at the lab in fifteen minutes. I'm feeding the rats and mice at I.B.L. over the summer," he explained.

He waited, expecting Cristina to say "Yech," or otherwise show some disgust for the rodents. But all she said was, "Neat."

"Now you come back again," Mrs. Sanchez ordered as she walked him to the door. "Don't think that just because there's no Casey to walk, you have to stay away." Her voice dropped to a whisper. "I'd hate for Cristina to get bored and decide she wants to go home early," she whispered. "It's such a comfort for me, having her here. You understand."

Scott nodded. He understood. But as he pedaled away, he wished Mrs. Sanchez wouldn't leave it up to him to keep Cristina happy enough to stay through the summer. The only thing he did well around Cristina was eat and blush. Could he build an entire summer around that?

Chapter Six

Every day Scott visited the pound, hoping Casey would show up. On the fifth day the answer was still the same. No Casey. At least whoever adopted him likes him, Scott decided, pedaling away from the pound and heading for the lab.

Usually it was pretty quiet around the I.B.L. building when Scott arrived. Today, three people were standing outside, holding signs in the air and chanting about saving something. Scott's thoughts were so full of Casey, though, he didn't pay much attention to their words or their signs. He didn't even notice the dirty looks they shot him as he went up the steps and in the door.

He checked in, then started his rounds, looking carefully at the rats with bandages on their backs. Was that lump underneath Joe's patch a tumor? Scott hoped not. He didn't like to think of Joe growing tumors so that Scott's mother could wear lipstick.

Scott made his rounds silently, no longer noticing the sound of the dogs behind the door. Day by day their barking had faded into the background. He was glad of that. They reminded him of Casey. He still felt like crying when he thought of Casey, but knowing the dog had been adopted helped.

The sign people were still outside when he left. This time he read their posters: FREE THE ANIMALS! END ANIMAL EXPERIMENTATION! ANIMALS HAVE RIGHTS! At the bottom of each sign were the words Animal Rights Front. Then, in brackets, A.R.F.

One of the people—a burly middle-aged man with a fringe of hair around his balding head—marched up to Scott and thrust his nose almost against Scott's. Scott backed off, but the man followed. "Vivisectionist!" he snarled.

Scott didn't know what the word meant, but he recognized the man's tone. Hostile. Definitely hostile. He backed up another step, but again the man followed.

Without even thinking, Scott said, as loud as he could, "ARF, ARF!"

Worry, he told himself later. Worry could be blamed for a lot of terrible things that happened to people or that people did. Perhaps it was the worry of losing Casey and having that nasty man snarl at him that made him say that.

The man's eyes nearly bugged out of his head. He looked over at his companions. "Can you believe it?" he asked. "Jokes. He makes jokes about our name."

One of the others, a young woman with short blond hair and a turned-up nose, hurried over. "Lay off, Peter. He's only a kid. For all you know, he hasn't a clue what a vivisectionist is."

"Ignorance is no excuse," Peter sneered. "Especially if you've been inside." He tipped his head toward the lab.

"You'll catch more flies with honey than with vin-

33

egar," the woman told the man. She walked up to Scott. "Hi," she said, "I'm Marcy. Do you know someone who works here?"

Scott nodded. "*I* do."

"What's your name?" Marcy asked.

Scott told her.

"Well, Scott, do you know what vivisection is?"

When Scott shook his head, she continued. "It's another name for animal experimentation—using animals in research. A.R.F. thinks animals shouldn't be used for research."

"Why not?"

"We believe it's cruel and violates the animals' rights. We believe there are other ways to do the experiments that don't torture living creatures."

Torture living creatures? Was he, Scott Richmond, torturing living creatures? Scott shook his head. "I only feed the rats and mice," he explained.

"And what are the animals you feed being used for?"

"Skin tests mostly. For lipstick."

"They clear a patch of skin and smear something on it?" asked Marcy.

Scott nodded.

"Aha!" snorted Peter to the third person, a thin, elderly woman with large, red-framed glasses, who had come over to listen. He thrust his face toward Scott again. "And do you know how they get the hair off that patch of skin in the first place?" he asked. Then, not waiting for an answer, he said, "They plaster a piece of adhesive tape to the rodent, then rip it off. The hair comes off too. Then sometimes they'll do it again and rip off the first layer of skin, so whatever chemical they're testing can go right onto raw flesh."

34

Scott felt the blood rush out of his head. He looked at Marcy. "That true?"

Marcy nodded. "That's often the way it's done."

Scott shivered, even though the day had turned hot. I'll quit, he told himself. Computer or no computer, I'll quit. No way would he work for a company that tortured animals.

Then he thought again. How did he know these people were telling the truth? They might say anything to gain support for their cause. After all, he'd been in the lab and he'd never seen anyone using adhesive tape to rip hair off rats. As a matter of fact, the animals had it easy, as far as he could tell. They lived in clean cages and had lots of food, water, and companionship. Soft City.

As though she had read his thoughts, Marcy said, "All we ask is that you keep your eyes open. Then you can make up your own mind."

Scott nodded, then took a step toward his bike.

Marcy put a hand on his arm. He noticed that her nails were unpolished and chewed short. "If you do learn something that upsets you or makes you think we're right, don't fly off the handle and quit, eh?" she said gently. "We could use a pair of eyes inside."

Spy! She was asking him to spy for them. To fill them in on all the dirty details of what went on in the lab. No way! Scott decided, as he shook off her hand and started toward his bike. Dr. Wilder was Tim's uncle and he'd been nice enough to give Scott a summer job. So no way was he going to spy on his boss. Scott wasn't perfect, but he had a few good qualities he prided himself on. One was loyalty. He didn't rat on his friends.

Scott unlocked his bike as quickly as he could,

35

anxious to put the protestors behind him. But as he jerked the lock open, Marcy said, "Think of the dogs, Scott. Those dogs you hear aren't howling from happiness."

Darn her! Scott thought, as he yanked the bike out of the rack. Why'd she have to go and say that? He'd managed to make himself immune to the barking. It had become like the ticking of his bedside clock, a sound that faded into the background unless he reminded himself to listen. And now Marcy's words had done just that—reminded him to listen.

The dog sounds moved to the front of his awareness, and for the first time in days, Scott heard them, really heard them. And what he heard made his stomach clench and his heart feel as though it were being squeezed into a shriveled ball. He listened again, certain his ears were playing tricks on him. But no, there it was, his trademark sound: kind of high-pitched and wheezy, as though a dog with a lisp had the sneezes but was still trying to bark. It was a sound Scott would know anywhere. Casey.

Chapter Seven

Although his first instinct was to charge into the lab and ask to see the dogs, Scott was unable to move. He felt as though his toenails had suddenly grown two feet long and embedded themselves in the ground.

Go! he told himself. Go! Check it out. You could be wrong. Maybe it isn't Casey. Maybe you only think it's Casey because you miss him so much.

Marcy must have noticed something was wrong. She took a few steps toward him and asked, "You okay?"

Scott nodded, though he still felt gut shot. Slowly he swung a leg over his bike, trying to look casual, while his mind searched for an answer. Do something, he ordered himself as he pedaled slowly through the parking lot toward the lane. Don't run away. Do something!

What would Marcy think if he went back into the lab? That he was going to tell Dr. Wilder they'd tried to recruit him to spy on his operation, that's what. And Peter? He might do more than stick his nose in Scott's face. Maybe going back in *wasn't* the right thing to do. But he had to do something.

No, he decided. Think, don't act. Going back into the lab and creating a ruckus was not a good idea. He had to take his time. He had to think about what he was going to do next. If that was Casey in there—and Scott would have bet his last dollar that it was—he didn't dare make any mistakes. Didn't dare rush into anything. He wasn't Indiana Jones. He was only a twelve-year-old kid. A twelve-year-old kid who had to save Casey.

By the time he reached his house, Scott had decided to tell his mother everything. She'd know what to do. Maybe a simple phone call to Dr. Wilder would be all it took to get Casey out of the lab. Thank you, brain, for thinking of that, Scott muttered, as he dropped his bike on the lawn, unlocked the front door as fast as he could, and dashed into the house.

"Mom!" Scott bellowed. "Mom! Where are you?"

No answer.

Scott groaned. He'd forgotten. It was grocery-shopping day.

Sit down. Wait. Be patient, Scott ordered, flinging himself onto the sofa. But he couldn't do it. He felt too jittery, as though a burglar alarm were ringing deep inside him. He couldn't sit and do nothing. Not while Casey was locked up inside that lab waiting to get his hair ripped off—or worse. He had to do *something*. He had to tell *someone*.

Tim! He'd tell Tim. Perhaps, between the two of them, they could figure out what to do. Scott shoved himself off the sofa and started toward the door.

As Scott pedaled his bike toward Tim's, a picture flashed into his head of Casey, a monstrous tumor bulging from his back. Dr. Wilder stood over him holding a glinting scalpel in his hand. Why, Dr.

Wilder's nothing but a murderer, he thought in alarm. Murderer! Murderer! Murderer! he screamed silently, and pedaled even faster, as though the violent spinning of his legs would fling the picture out of his mind.

Suddenly Scott braked to a halt. He couldn't tell Tim. Dr. Wilder was Tim's uncle. How could he tell his best friend that his uncle was about to perform some disgusting test on Casey? Either Tim wouldn't believe him or, if he did, he'd be so upset he'd never speak to his uncle again. And most likely never speak to Scott again either, since he had been the bearer of the bad news.

Yet Scott's throat ached with the need to tell someone. His discovery was too painful to hold inside.

Mrs. Sanchez! She'd need to know. And perhaps she'd even have an idea of what to do. Scott started pedaling, this time toward Mrs. Sanchez's house. Then he again skidded to a stop.

Scott said a nasty word under his breath. I must have fed my brain to the lab rats, he thought. I can't tell Mrs. Sanchez that Casey is in the lab waiting to be experimented on. She'd think it was her fault and feel like a monster. A great lump of sadness and anger welled up in him, caught in the back of his throat, and threatened to choke him. The anger won.

It *is* her fault, he told himself. If she hadn't sent Casey to the pound, he wouldn't be in this fix now. She *should* feel rotten!

But it was Scott who felt rotten as soon as he thought that—if it were possible to feel more rotten than he already did.

"Aw, cripes!" he muttered, leaning heavily on his bike handlebars. There was no way he could tell Mrs.

39

Sanchez. No way was he going to do that to her. Then he straightened. No, he couldn't tell Mrs. Sanchez. But there was someone he could talk to—Mrs. Sanchez's niece Cristina.

Scott hadn't seen Cristina since that first day. He'd been too busy checking the pound for Casey and working, he'd told himself.

Do I really want to listen to more of her smart talk? he wondered now. I'm not even certain what she'll be able to do. He started to wheel his bike around to head home, then changed his mind. If I don't talk to someone about this soon, I'm going to explode, he decided, and headed for Mrs. Sanchez's.

Cristina was sweeping the front porch when Scott rode up. He took a deep breath, then whispered, as loudly as he dared, "I've got to talk to you."

Cristina scrunched her eyebrows together. "Huh?" she asked.

"I've got to talk to you. It's about Casey."

"What about Casey?"

"For cripe's sake, don't talk so loud. I don't want your aunt to hear what I have to tell you."

Cristina's dark eyes, only seconds before as black as thunderheads, now sparked with interest. "So, tell."

"Casey's at I.B.L.," Scott said, then went on to tell Cristina all he knew.

Cristina's eyes got wider and wider as he talked. "O-o-o-o-o-o-wee!" she said, when Scott finished his explanation. "You sure about all this?"

Scott shrugged. "Pretty sure. I know it sounded just like Casey's bark. He has this real weird bark that goes—"

Cristina cut him off. "I know how it goes."

40

"How could you know?" Scott asked. "Casey was already gone to the pound when you got here."

Cristina rolled her eyes and looked disgusted. "I've visited *Tia* before, you know."

"Then why haven't I ever seen you?"

It was Cristina's turn to shrug. "Not very observant, I suppose."

Scott let her remark pass. There were more important things to think about than how annoying Cristina Martinez could be.

"So what's the plan?" Cristina asked.

"The plan?" Scott wrinkled his nose at the girl.

"Well, obviously you need to save Casey. I figured that since you told me about him, you must have some plan to save him and that you need my help to carry it off."

Scott's head dropped. "A plan. A plan," he muttered under his breath into his shirt buttons. Then he lifted his head. "My plan is to tell my parents," he explained. "Then they'll phone Dr. Wilder and explain the situation and he'll let Casey go. Nothing to it."

Cristina shook her head. "No, no, no," she said. "All wrong. Brother, you'd make a lousy investigative reporter. Don't you know you're supposed to collect all your ammunition before you aim the big guns? You're not even certain it's Casey in there. What if you mouth off and then find out it isn't him? What kind of smart ass would that make you?"

A stupid smart ass, Scott thought, although he'd never admit that to Cristina, who probably thought he had bubble gum for brains.

"I wasn't planning to mouth off before I found out for sure," he explained, although he would have told his mother if she'd been home. Luckily Cristina didn't know that. "That's why I'm talking to you, not to your aunt or my parents," he continued. "You don't have to be so snippy about it." He started cracking the knuckles of his right hand.

"Okay, okay," said Cristina, raising her palms to him. "Just quit with that disgusting noise."

"Sorry," said Scott. "I do that when I'm nervous. Okay," he went on, "as soon as I get to work tomorrow I'll find out if it's really Casey."

"Tomorrow? Can't you find out today?"

Scott thought about going back to the lab. "I can't go back today," he said, and explained about the A.R.F. pickets and how they might think he was ratting on them.

"Well, what about tonight?"

"At night?" Scott was so surprised at her suggestion, his voice went into a high squeak. He shook his head. "I don't have a key—and I'm not going to break in."

Cristina curled her lip. "Boy, you really would make a lousy reporter," she sneered.

"That's fine with me," Scott snapped, "because I don't intend to be one." His hands eased into their knuckle-snapping position. He shoved them deep into his pockets.

"Good," said Cristina.

Scott's feelings still stung from Cristina's remarks. Then he realized she was right. If there was a way to find out that night if Casey was in the lab, he should do it. "Maybe I'd better go tonight," he said then.

"Great! What time do you want me to meet you?"

"Meet me? What for?"

"So I can go with you, of course. Do you think I'd

let a story like this get by me? It'll be an adventure. I lo-o-o-ve ad-*ven*-tures."

It was Scott's turn to shake his head. "I don't think your brain is firing on all cylinders."

"Don't be a wimp," Cristina ordered. "I'm coming whether you want me to or not, so you might as well give me all the details. First, how are you going to get in?"

"I'm not going to get in," Scott explained. "This is what I'm going to do." When he finished describing his plan to Cristina, he added, "Meet me here at midnight—if your aunt will let you out of the house."

"No *problema. Tia*'s usually asleep before nine. And I like your plan."

Scott grinned. "See you later then," he said.

As he climbed on his bike, Cristina gave him a thumbs-up signal. "Midnight. And don't worry. Together, nothing can stop us."

Chapter Eight

"That you, Scott?" called his mother, when Scott got home a few minutes later to find bags of groceries squatting on the kitchen floor.

"Yo-o."

"Would you put the rest of those groceries away? Julie has a fever and I'm going to sponge her off. I think I got most of the frozen stuff, but you'd better check."

Brother, that kid can find more ways to get attention, Scott thought, as he began to empty bags. "You missed the ice cream," he called up the stairs. He pried off the lid and saw that the outside layer looked runny. "Nothing worse than refrozen chocolate chip ice cream," he muttered to himself, heading for a spoon.

When all the grocery bags were empty and stashed in the garage, Scott headed upstairs. He found his red-faced, dopey-eyed sister sitting beside the sink while his mother wiped her down.

Julie raised one limp finger and whispered, "Hi, Hot Scott."

"What's the matter?" Scott asked, sorry for his

earlier thought that Julie was using the fever simply to get more attention. The kid really did look sick.

His mother shrugged. "I've made a doctor's appointment for first thing in the morning. I suppose she's getting a cold. Julie always spikes a fever before her nose starts to run." She pulled a nightie over Julie's head and bundled her into her arms. "Okay, sweetie," she said, "let's get you into bed."

Scott was glad Julie's nightie covered her down to her toes. In spite of how she ticked him off all the time, the sight of the bites and bruises on her matchstick legs twisted his heart.

It was what Scott called a messy evening. His father came home late from his job as service manager at a car dealership. Dinner was whatever anyone felt like grabbing, since his mother was busy running back and forth to check on Julie. He knew his mother and father would be doing that the whole night.

First time I ever try to sneak out of the house and it has to be a night when everyone is on the prowl, Scott thought. I'll have to time my escape perfectly.

Scott gave the dogs a long walk, then went to his room at his usual bedtime, glad he'd taken to closing his door. That way his parents wouldn't miss him unless they opened it to say good night. He hoped they'd be too busy with Julie.

Scott read for a while, then decided to listen to the radio until it was time to sneak out for his midnight meeting with Cristina. But first he timed his parent's trips into Julie's room. Every twenty to thirty minutes. That made it easy to get out. He only hoped he didn't run into one of them on the way back in.

He looked at the clock. Ten. It had to be later than

that. He flicked the clock with his finger. Move faster, he silently ordered the hands, then settled back as the radio started to play some mushy love song.

The next time Scott checked the clock it read 12:05. 12:05?! His body seemed to lift straight up off the bed. Then his feet hit the floor. He must have fallen asleep. What a butt head! How could he have let that happen? Cristina would think he'd chickened out.

Scott started to open his door when he realized he didn't know when his parents had made their last trip to Julie's room. He had to chance it. If he ran into one of them, he'd pretend he was sleepwalking.

The door to his parents' room was open and a small lamp on the dresser glowed. He peeked around the doorjamb. They were lying on their backs, but Scott couldn't tell if they were asleep.

In two silent steps he was past the door and on his way downstairs. Moments later he was pushing his bike silently away from the house.

Scott had never been out this late alone before. It was weird. Everything was quiet, and except for a few yard and streetlights and a lighted window here and there, everything stood in blackness. Then a dog barked. Scott's skin prickled. For a second he'd almost forgotten why he was prowling around in the middle of the night.

Quickly he swung his leg over his bike and headed toward the meeting place. He hoped Cristina was still there.

She was. "Thought you'd chickened out," she whispered, tapping her watch.

"I fell asleep."

"Nerves of steel. Who'da thunk it?" This time her whisper was sarcastic.

"I'm not getting much sleep lately," Scott retorted. "I spend most of the night worrying about Casey. I just hope I can get back in the house okay." He told Cristina about Julie's fever.

"Come on," he said then. "Let's get this over with. Where's your bike?"

"Bike? I don't have a bike."

"Holy taco! How do you think you're going to get there? If I'd known that, I wouldn't have let you come."

"You're not *letting* me come," Cristina snapped. "I don't need your permission. And it's only six blocks. You can ride me." She started to hop onto the cross bar in front of the seat.

"Not there," Scott said quickly. "You can sit on the handlebars. Then we won't be so . . . so . . . lopsided."

"How will you see where you're going?"

"I know where I'm going. Besides, it's so dark I can't see much even without you blocking my view."

They teetered off, Cristina balanced precariously on the handlebars and Scott trying in vain to keep from butting his head against her back whenever he had to pedal up a slight incline.

Scott stopped the bike partway down the lane leading toward I.B.L., about a half block away. "We'll walk from here," he whispered, then hid the bike behind some bushes.

Except for the quiet scuffle of a sneaker every now and then and the hopeful croaking of a lone frog, there wasn't a sound.

At the end of the lane, a driveway led into the parking lot in front of the building, which sat alone in a grove of isolated eucalyptus trees. A single street-light shone at the driveway entrance. About fifty yards down the driveway, Scott cut left through the trees, and in a few minutes they came out at the far edge of the lawn at the side of the building. Scott pointed to some hawthorn bushes and they squatted down behind them.

"Better reconnoiter first," Cristina whispered, "just to be sure there's no security guard."

Security guard? Scott hadn't even thought of that. "Why would there be a guard?" he asked.

"Because of the demonstrations, dodo. What if that bunch of crazies decided to blow up the lab?"

Scott snorted. It came out louder than he had intended. "Those people aren't crazy." Then he thought of Peter almost nose to nose with him and talking mean. "Well, most of them aren't."

Scott was about to stand up and saunter over to the building, just to prove to Cristina how dumb he thought she was for suggesting there might be a guard, when a car, headlights off, drove quietly into the parking lot in front of I.B.L.

Scott and Cristina plastered themselves face first on the grass behind the hawthorns. Scott's heart was pounding so loud in his ears he could scarcely hear the sound the engine made as the car coasted to a stop beside the front entrance.

"Who is it?" Cristina whispered. From the flutter in her voice, Scott could tell she was as frightened as he.

"Can't tell," he whispered back, not letting on that the reason he couldn't was because his eyes were squeezed shut with fright. Then he realized he'd better open them, if only to see which way to run. So he raised his head a couple of inches and peered out be-

tween his scrinched eyelids, not knowing who he'd
see, the police or a mad A.R.F. bomber. Not knowing
who he'd *prefer* to see, the police or a mad bomber.
The police, he decided immediately. A mad bomber
might blow up Casey—or him, come to think of it.

The car door opened. Scott heard Cristina suck in
her breath and hold it. At the same time she seemed
to sink lower into the grass. The dome light went on
in the car and Scott saw a khaki shirt. A boot clunked
onto the pavement and Scott saw a khaki pant leg.
Then he noticed the shield on the door.

"It's a rent-a-cop," he whispered as the shadowy
form stood up, hitched his pants, rested a hand on his
gun holster, and looked around. The guard walked toward the front door and disappeared from view.

"Let's get out of here," Scott whispered.

"You go if you want," Cristina hissed. "I'm hanging around to see what happens."

She's nuts, Scott told himself, and was about to
scramble to his feet and dash away without her when
he thought about Casey waiting in the dark building.
As he settled into the grass again, he thought he heard
Cristina sigh in a relieved sort of way. For certain he
felt the look she shot him in the dark. He imagined it
was a relieved sort of look.

They heard the rattle of a handle as the guard tried
the front door that led into the reception area and of-
fices. Then they heard his footsteps head toward the
corner of the building, toward *their* side of the building. Another handle rattled, this time on the door
Scott used when he came to work, the door leading
directly into the rodent room. Scott knew there was
another door around the back, and another around the
far side, which meant, if the guard was going to try

49

all the doors, he'd pass within fifty feet of them—unless he went back and forth on the far side of the building.

Scott pressed himself lower into the lawn. The grass was damp from an early evening sprinkling and had a sharp, tangy smell, as though it had been recently spread with chemical fertilizer. Scott hoped he didn't end up like the lab rats, with a chemical burn on his skin. He wondered if the chemical in the fertilizer had been tested on animals before it was tested on grass. Then he wondered how he could be thinking about such things when any second the security guard with the gun on his belt might come around the corner of the building, see him, and blow him away.

A few seconds later the guard did come around the corner, flashing his light into the bushes that hugged the building wall as he silently followed the lawn around to the back door.

One swing of the light our way and we're goners, Scott thought. If that happens, will I run for it or stand up with my hands in the air? He couldn't decide.

Crack! The sound slammed Scott's breath right out of him. He didn't know where it had come from, didn't know where to look for the source. Then he realized his hands had crept together and were clenched in their knuckle-cracking position. In the night quiet, the noise seemed as loud as a gunshot, and Scott was certain the guard would be on them in a nanosecond.

At that moment the guard's light darted across the grass toward their hiding place.

As the guard's light came closer, Scott felt a lump in his stomach like he'd eaten too many Gummi

Worms. Only the lump inside him wasn't Gummi Worms. It was fear.

The flashlight played over the leaves of the hawthorns. Where it went after that, Scott didn't see because he shut his eyes again, knowing when he opened them he would be staring at the shiny black toes of the guard's boots.

Then Scott heard the faint rattle of the back door handle and he realized the guard had gone past them and they were safe. Scott opened his mouth and sucked in air, the sweetest, freshest air he had ever tasted.

A couple of minutes later, the guard, having continued on around the building, was back at the car, talking loudly into his radio.

"Looks quiet," he said. "I'll make another swing by later."

Scott heard Cristina blow a long, quiet breath into the grass. His heart was thumping again, so hard he was surprised it wasn't jolting his whole body slightly off the grass with every beat.

When the car had driven quietly away, they both got to their feet and ran toward the building. Neither said a word, as though not talking about the guard would turn him into a bad dream they had unexpectedly shared.

I.B.L. was a boxy, one-story brick building. Except for the front office area, the only windows were high, small ones near the twelve-foot ceilings, that were opened from inside by a long pole with a hook on the end. Those windows were covered with a metal grill on the outside. So they can leave the windows open and not worry about anyone breaking in, Scott supposed. Or the animals breaking out.

51

Tonight, a couple of windows were open a crack. One was toward the front of the building, where Scott knew the rodent room was. The other was toward the middle. It was this window he headed for.

"I'm glad it's quiet," Scott whispered. It was the first time either had spoken since the guard left. "I was worried that it would be as noisy as it is during the daytime."

"Maybe the animals don't make any noise if they know there's no one to hear," Cristina replied.

"If we don't shut up they'll know *we're* here," Scott said, "and then we won't learn a thing from all this creeping around."

"So do your thing," Cristina whispered.

"First, boost me up," Scott ordered. "I want to get as close to the window as I can."

"How do you expect me to do that?"

"Let me get on your shoulders. It'll just be for a second."

"Okay. Okay." Cristina knelt down and steadied herself against the wall among the azalea bushes while Scott climbed onto her shoulders.

"You could have taken off your shoes," she complained as she wobbled to her feet.

"And leave them behind as evidence if we have to make a run for it?" Scott hissed down at her. "No way. Now be quiet," he added.

Even with Scott on Cristina's shoulders, the window was still about three feet above Scott's head. He tilted his head back, puckered his lips and whistled. Four notes. First a high note. Then a low note. Then a repeat. Casey's whistle.

Scott held his breath. He knew that if Casey were in the lab he'd bark when he heard that whistle. And if they were lucky, Casey would sound off before the other dogs, so they'd know for sure it was him.

Two heartbeats worth of silence followed Scott's whistle. Then all hell broke loose. Scott jumped off Cristina's shoulders and cocked his ear toward the window.

Every dog barking had its own distinctive sound. Scott heard high-pitched barks, wheezy barks, and lispy barks. Even sneezy barks. But none combined to make a sound exactly like Casey's. A couple were close, but not close enough.

Scott realized Cristina was staring at him, her eyebrows raised. He shook his head. He didn't know if he should laugh or cry.

Cristina jerked her head toward the road. "Let's get out of here. That noise might bring the guard back."

Once away from the building, Scott slowed to a walk. "I guess I was wrong," he muttered. "I guess I didn't hear Casey this afternoon."

"But that's good, isn't it? That means he really was adopted and has a new home."

"I guess so," Scott said.

He mustn't have sounded very convinced, because Cristina added, "It's better than him being in the lab, isn't it? Now you won't have to figure out a way to rescue him and you don't have to worry about him being experimented on. And aren't you glad you didn't tell your parents and have them phone Dr. Wilder?"

Scott felt a bit better. "Yeah," he agreed. "That would have gotten things in an uproar all right. And all for nothing. I probably would have gotten fired.

"Do you realize," he continued, "that if that guard

had come a few seconds later, he would have caught us by the building?"

"Yeah. It was a close call anyway with you cracking your stupid knuckles. You know, that's a really dumb habit."

Scott kicked at a black lump on the ground. It mushed. He dragged the toe of his sneaker through some grass. "Yeah. I guess it is a dumb habit," he agreed.

"Anyway," he went on, "even with the guard scaring me out of my toenails, I'm glad I stuck around."

"Me, too," said Cristina. "I thought you were going to take off on me."

"I was going to take off. Then I thought about Casey. Anyway," he added with a laugh, "I don't think my legs would have held me up." It was the first time he remembered laughing since Casey had been gone. Cripes, it felt good.

Cristina laughed too. "I don't think my legs would have held me up either," she said. "They felt like two stalks of overcooked asparagus."

They had reached the bush where Scott had hidden his bike. He stopped. "Don't tell anyone about what we did tonight," he said. "It's got to be kept quiet."

Cristina gave a disgusted squawk. "What do you take me for? A burp brain? And who would I tell anyway? *Tia?*"

Scott retrieved his bike from behind the bushes. "I was just thinking about it, that's all," Scott explained. Why did the girl have to jump on him every time he tried to tell her something? "Like, you haven't met my friend Tim yet, but if you do, it's really important that he doesn't know I thought Casey was at the lab."

Scott held the bike steady while Cristina hopped

onto the handlebars. "Why shouldn't he know? If he's your best friend and all."

"Because his uncle runs the place," Scott explained.

"'Nuff said," Cristina said. "I get the picture. Zip my lip around Tim." She squirmed on the handlebars. "I'm glad we don't do this often. It could get a little hard on my behind—and my poor, stepped-on shoulders."

"It's a little hard on my nerves," joked Scott. "Say," he said then, serious again, "you don't think it was Casey I heard this afternoon and that we didn't hear him tonight because . . . because . . ." He couldn't bring himself to finish.

"Naw," Cristina reassured him, guessing at what was on his mind. "I'm sure most of those lab animals are kept alive for a long time. Otherwise, how would they get any test results?"

"Yeah," sighed Scott, relieved. "You're probably right. If Casey was there, he'd still be alive and we would have heard him bark. I guess those people who adopted him really like him and aren't going to give him up. I guess I should quit worrying about him. But I won't quit missing him. He was the best dog I ever knew."

Chapter Nine

"Want to come over for some *one–on–one* after breakfast?" Scott had asked Tim over the phone the next morning. He had made it into the house without getting caught, had slept like a lump of concrete, and was feeling pumped. Now he was ready for some food and some exercise. Meanwhile, his mother was scurrying about getting Julie ready for her doctor's appointment and giving Scott instructions at the same time.

"Eat up the rest of that cantaloupe, okay?" she said, dashing through the kitchen as Scott poured himself a bowl of Corn Crunchies.

"Sure, Mom," Scott answered.

"And please tidy that pigpen you call a bedroom," she called over her shoulder a few minutes later as she headed up the stairs.

"Sure, Mom," Scott said again, digging a spoon into his melon. With luck, she'd forget she'd mentioned cleaning his room and he could skip it for another week. Then he forgot everything—his mother, his room, everything—when he noticed Marcy's picture staring at him from the morning paper. She was holding up her sign that said ANIMALS HAVE RIGHTS! Peering over her shoulder were Peter and the older woman.

A.R.F. WANTS LIBERATION IN THE LABS screamed the headline. Then came the article:

"Nearly 100 million animals die every year in our nation's laboratories," claims Animal Rights Front member, Marcy Niven. "While advances in medicine *have* been made using animals in research," said Niven, "many of the tests performed are useless or unnecessary. A.R.F. supports the search for new methods of research to replace those cruel, inhumane methods now in use. More work such as that currently being done at the Johns Hopkins Center for Alternatives to Animal Testing is needed."

One of more than 400 active animal rights groups in this country campaigning for more ethical treatment of animals, A.R.F. began picketing the Institute for Better Living yesterday and plans to continue doing so until the public has been made aware of the ongoing activities of this local, private research laboratory.

Great, thought Scott. I'll have to put up with Peter and his snarling every day. He continued to read.

When asked to name specific tests conducted by I.B.L. that A.R.F. objects to, Niven cited the Lethal Dose 50 test, during which substances are injected under the skin or into the stomach of test subjects until half of the animals have died. Also mentioned was the Draize test in which the eyes of immobilized subjects are smeared with products to be tested. Rabbits are

57

the test subject of choice since they make no tears and cannot wash the foreign substance out of their eyes.

Scott's mouth was still chewing and swallowing melon, but his stomach was threatening to toss it back. Lethal Dose 50 test? Draize test? Were things like that going on at I.B.L.? Thank goodness Casey wasn't there. He swallowed hard before reading on.

While unsure if either of these tests are being employed at I.B.L. at this time, Niven claimed an unnamed source told her that "inhumane" skin tests are currently being conducted to determine the safety of a product to be used in lipstick.

Scott's stomach knotted around his cantaloupe when he read that. There was no doubt in his mind who the "unnamed source" was. It was him, Scott Richmond.

After that, Scott wasn't certain what the article said, his eyes were so blurred with shock. Something about A.R.F. preferring peaceful protest, but not being opposed to making a stronger statement. Something about alternative methods of research. The only word Scott understood in *that* bunch was *cadaver.* He knew that was a dead body. The rest of it boggled his mind.

"Is that the article about I.B.L. you're reading?" Scott's mother asked on her way through the kitchen again. "If that kind of demonstration is going on, I'm not sure you should keep working there. Some of those groups can get pretty nasty. The article says one organization even broke into a university lab and stole some of the research animals."

"There are only three people protesting," Scott explained. "One man was kind of mean, but the younger woman in the picture was pretty nice. And the article says they're a peaceful protest group." Scott didn't mention that Marcy had asked him to spy for them.

"Well, you watch it, okay? Don't get in their way. After all, if you're working there, they might consider you a target. If anything happens to upset you, anything at all, you hustle right home and tell me about it. Promise?"

Scott nodded. His eyes had cleared enough by then that he could concentrate on the rest of the article.

Niven concluded by saying that A.R.F.'s next target will be the local pound, which continues to sell unclaimed animals to laboratories for research purposes.

So Casey could have wound up at the lab after all, Scott thought. The pound could have sold him to I.B.L. For the first time Scott was almost glad Casey had been adopted immediately.

But surely the pound would wait the full thirty days before selling an animal to a lab—to give it a chance to get adopted first, Scott thought. Even so, it was a rotten thing to do, to sell animals to a lab to get experimented on just because they didn't have a home. If I were a stray, I'd rather get run over by a car or have the pound kill me, Scott decided.

I wouldn't have thought that way a few days ago, Scott told himself as he headed to his room to dress. Then, all I knew about were the skin tests, which seem pretty tame. But now I know about the Draize and the Lethal Dose 50. Yuck!

It was then Scott made a decision. When Marcy and her A.R.F. group started picketing the pound, he,

Scott Richmond, would be there too—carrying a sign with the rest of them.

"Hey, Muttman," Tim said as he came through the door a while later, "let's go dunk a few."

"I'm ready," said Scott, although he had sort of lost his interest in basketball. He'd felt so full of energy when he'd gotten up that morning, and now, after reading that newspaper article, he was dragging.

"Hey, man, are we playing *one–on–one* or *one–on–nothing?*" Tim asked, when he'd run the score up to 14–2.

"Sorry," Scott said. "I can't keep my mind on the game."

"I guess you're still upset about Casey," Tim suggested, dribbling the ball through his legs and around his back.

"Yeah. I want to go back to the pound. Just to, ya know, double-check."

"You mean double-double-double-check, don't you?" Tim asked. "You've already been back five times. But, hey, maybe the people who adopted Casey decided this morning they don't want him and are bringing him back right this minute. It's worth a try." Tim hooked the ball toward the netless metal rim. It twanged off the metal and plopped back into Tim's hands.

Scott raised his arms in a halfhearted attempt to guard Tim. "Let's go now," he said.

Tim dropped the ball, clutched his throat, and fell to his knees. "Please, Your Majesty. A drink. A drink before our long journey."

"Oh, come on," said Scott, laughing and giving the ball a boot before heading into the house.

Inside, Scott grabbed a bottle of orange soda and two glasses. He poured, then handed one to Tim.

Tim peered into the glass with a frown. "Don't you *ever* use ice cubes?" he asked.

Scott shook his head. "Waters down the taste." He grabbed Tim's glass and walked to the fridge for ice. When he turned to hand it back, he found Tim bent over the newspaper, which Scott had left lying on the table.

"Wow!" Tim said, pushing his glasses up onto his nose. "My uncle's lab! I knew something was going on there because I heard my parents talking, but I didn't know what. Was it on the TV, too?" Tim's family didn't subscribe to a newspaper or own a television.

Tim started to read the article. "Was all this going on when you were at work yesterday? What was it like? Was it scary?"

"Not half as scary as what's in that article," Scott said, not certain it was a good idea to let Tim read the article, but making no move to stop him.

"Oh," Tim said quietly, when he had read the part about the tests. "I didn't know my uncle did this kind of stuff. My parents always talk like what my uncle does is wonderful because the things he learns might save lives. They never mentioned these rotten tests."

Suddenly feeling sorry for his friend and wishing he'd put away the paper, Scott said, "We don't know that your uncle does those tests. The only test A.R.F. even knows about for sure is that skin test."

"Yeah," Tim said. "I wonder who the unnamed source is? It must be someone who works in the lab. Boy, I wouldn't want to be that person if my uncle finds out he squealed."

Scott sucked soda up his nose and started coughing.

Tim slapped him on the back without taking his eyes off the newspaper. "All these other tests A.R.F. wants to use instead," he continued, when Scott could breathe again. "Computer assays? Simulated tissues? Mass spectrometry? What *is* all that?"

Scott shrugged. "At least you can say the words," he said. "I couldn't even do that—much less tell you what the tests are all about."

Tim finished the article. "Come on," he said. "We'd better get to the pound right away, just in case Casey has been returned. You wouldn't want him to be sold to the lab."

"That's for sure," Scott agreed, wondering what Tim would think if he knew what Scott had been through the night before.

"I think I'll ask my mom about all that stuff when I get home," Tim said as they pedaled off.

"But then she'll know you've been reading the newspaper."

"That's okay. She reads it at work all the time. Some days, she even tells my father what she read. He pretends not to listen, but I know he does. Afterward he always gives us his little spiel though: 'People today are bombarded by more information than their poor brains can process,'" Tim shouted, imitating his father. " 'Do you know we get more information from one daily newspaper than a person a few centuries ago got in his entire lifetime? Get rid of television! Get rid of newspapers! Get rid of magazines!'

"Every time my dad says, 'Give your brain a

break,' " Tim continued, "my mother says, 'If you live in a vacuum, you'll only blow hot air.' "

"What does that mean?" asked Scott.

"I think it means if you don't know what's going on in the world, you won't have anything intelligent to talk about. Like, I should know about this stuff at the lab and I wouldn't have known if I hadn't read the paper."

"Be sure and tell me what your mom says," Scott panted, pedaling toward the pound and hoping, hoping, hoping, this time Casey would be there.

Chapter Ten

Scott tried not to feel too disappointed when he and Tim once again didn't find Casey at the pound. Keeping busy helped, so, on the way back home, he convinced Tim to give him a hand tidying up his room for the first time that summer. It took them over an hour to sort the Lego pieces, pick up dirty clothes that smelled like sauerkraut, and haul the moldy dishes and paper cups down to the kitchen. But after Tim went home for lunch, Scott felt at loose ends, like an arrow with no target in sight.

His mother and Julie hadn't come home from the doctor's, so Scott headed for I.B.L. early.

There were more protestors than the day before, Scott noticed, as he chained his bike and spun the combination lock—probably because of the publicity in the paper. Some A.R.F. members had brought dogs with them. One dog had a sign over its back that read THE GREATNESS OF A NATION AND ITS MORAL PROGRESS CAN BE JUDGED BY THE WAY ITS ANIMALS ARE TREATED.——MAHATMA GANDHI. The other dog had a sign that read, I WAS RESCUED FROM MEDICAL RESEARCHERS.

More people milling around outside meant more confusion, so Scott was able to slip up to the lab door without being stopped or questioned. He had to knock for Jackson to let him in though, because, for the first time, the door was locked.

The dogs seemed quieter today, as though they knew they had some champions outside who were rooting for them and they could therefore save their own energy for staying alive.

Jackson answered the door with his usual bottle of Coca-Cola uptilted to his mouth. Whenever he came near Scott, Scott was certain he could hear the pop sloshing around in Jackson's stomach, like well water sloshing in a bucket. Scott knew Jackson was trying to quit his Coke habit and was bringing only two large bottles to work with him every day. By the time Scott arrived, Jackson was usually on his second bottle and would nurse it through the rest of his shift. From the looks of this bottle, it wasn't going to last that long today though.

"I see you made it through the line of bleedin'-heart animal lovers," Jackson said when he saw Scott.

Scott nodded. "They're shouting 'Wilder, come out.'"

"Tough bananas," snorted Jackson. "Wilder left day before yesterday for some convention. Won't be back for a couple of days. Maybe the watchdogs'll give up by then." He upended his bottle again and took a swig.

"I guess not many experiments go on when Dr. Wilder is out of town," Scott suggested.

Jackson shook his head, belched. "Wrong. Wilder isn't the only researcher in this place. He has assistants who do the experiments. I run the skin tests on

65

the rodents. Others do tests for . . ." Jackson paused as though realizing he might be talking out of turn. ". . . tests for other things," he finished, turning to go back to his cubicle.

Scott started his rounds. He worked slowly, wondering what kind of day he'd be having if Casey had answered his whistle last night. *I'd be figuring out a way to get into the restricted area,* he told himself.

"He'd barely gotten started when he heard Jackson say, "Aw-w-w! Just what I need." There was frantic scrambling and some foul language. Then Jackson came out of his office, his hand shoved deep into one pocket. "Hey, kid," he said, "do me a favor. Take a ride over to the corner market and get me a bottle of Coke. I just dumped my last one all over my desk, and the stupid pop machine in the front office is busted." He pulled a five-dollar bill out of his pocket and held it out to Scott.

"Sure," said Scott. He took the money and headed for the door. When he opened it he noticed there were a lot more people out there than when he arrived. And most of them didn't look—or sound—too happy.

"What's all that shoutin'?" Jackson asked, coming to peer over Scott's head. "Oh, great," he muttered. "Some kind of counterdemonstration."

"What's F.I.F.A.R.?" Scott asked, noticing the new signs.

"Formerly Ill for Animal Research," Jackson explained. "Former medical patients who support animal research. They say they'd be dead if it weren't for experiments on animals."

"What's the connection?" Scott asked.

"They were probably saved by some drug that was tested on animals first," Jackson explained.

66

"Oh, yeah, my mom mentioned research with animals saving lives. But that's just a few animals, right?"

Jackson snorted. *"Lots* of the animals in labs are used for medical research. A lot of new drugs are being tested all the time."

Scott shook his head as he watched Peter and a young man stand toe to toe and shout at each other. He didn't want to hear what they were saying. Just as he didn't want to hear what Jackson was saying. He didn't want to hear that something good might come out of torturing innocent animals like Casey.

"Besides, fewer cosmetic firms are usin' animals all the time," Jackson said then. "Ever hear of Cover Girl cosmetics?"

Scott shook his head.

"How about Noxema?"

This time Scott nodded. "Oh, yeah, my mom uses that to wash her face. And she puts it on us if we get a sunburn."

"The same company makes both Cover Girl and Noxema. And it's testin' new products on tissue samples 'stead of rabbits," Jackson explained. "It cut its use of test animals by about eighty percent. I heard Mary Kay cosmetics is gonna stop usin' animals, too, at least for a while."

So people like Marcy are doing some good, thought Scott, as he watched the young woman squaring off with a burly bear of a man who was shaking his fist in her face.

"Heatin' up out there," Jackson commented. A siren wailed in the distance. "Lucky Wilder isn't here. He'd be havin' a stroke. The lab doesn't need this kind of publicity." He reached around Scott and pulled the door closed. "Forget your bike. You better go out the back way. If you cut across the lawn and through the trees you come out near the store anyway."

Scott followed Jackson back toward his office. I get to go through the restricted area, he suddenly realized. Now that I don't have to get in there, I get a free tour. He shoved his hands into his pockets to keep his knuckles quiet.

When Jackson reached the door, he pulled a key out of his pocket. Even though the man went through the door all the time, this was the first time Scott had seen him unlock it first. He must have been blind not to notice before. Not blind, he told himself. Just not interested until now. He remembered how he had never noticed ads for computers until he had decided to buy one. Now he saw them everywhere.

"Straight down the hall, then right to the exit," Jackson explained, and the door clanged shut behind Scott.

The smell was stronger on this side of the door. More like a hospital. It didn't sound much like a hospital though. Although Scott could hear the faint voices of people talking, that sound was overshadowed by the whining, chattering, and mewing that spewed out of the doors on both sides of the hall.

If this is my only chance to see the rest of the lab, I'm going to see as much as possible, Scott decided, starting slowly down the hallway.

The first room on his left was filled with cages holding nothing but rabbits. There was one row of rabbits in odd wooden boxes with only their heads sticking out. A man in a white lab coat was spraying something into one rabbit's eye.

Scott's stomach flipped. Is that the Draize test? he wondered.

Scott had trouble seeing what was in the cages in the first room on his right. All he could see were quiet lumps of fur huddled in the cage corners. Maybe cats. Monkeys, too, he decided, when a screech pierced his eardrums.

From the few yelps and whines, he knew even before he came to the last room on the left that it was the dog room. Even through the closed door the odor of antiseptic stung his nose and made him want to hurry past, but he forced himself to stop. A sign hanging on the door said STERILE AREA. Scott wondered what that meant as he took a quick peek up and down the hall, then opened the door and slipped through.

On the opposite wall, up near the ceiling, was the open window Scott had whistled through the night before. A few tables were set up along the wall. About ten cages crouched against the wall to his right, some of them occupied. In the corner immediately to his left was a scrub sink. Beside the sink was a shelf full of hospital caps and gowns in plastic bags. A large trash can sat next to the sink. Scott could see the sleeve of a discarded paper gown hanging over the edge. The left side of the room was divided into five tiny cubicles with flimsy-looking walls. Each cubicle had a door with a window.

There was no one in the room with the animals, so Scott slipped farther into the room to take a good look. Some of the dogs in cages seemed to be asleep. Some looked pretty sick—skinny and missing patches of hair.

He moved to the door of the first cubicle. Like the hall door, it had a sign on it that read STERILE AREA.

69

A chart hanging beside the door said something about a test number and a subject number that didn't mean anything to Scott.

Scott looked toward the hall door, then peeked through the window in the cubicle to see a cage like the ones behind him. He peered at the animal curled up inside the cage and his heart almost stopped when he saw a swatch of gold. Casey! The dog lifted his head. No—a golden retriever. Scott breathed again.

Scott would never forget the look in the retriever's eyes. It was a look that pleaded for the freedom of a run in the park, a squirrel to chase, or a ball to fetch. It was a look Scott couldn't bear to see.

Quickly Scott backed away, slipped through the door, and hurried on down the hall. He turned right at the end, looked for an exit sign, and ran straight into a trolley cart being pushed down the hall by a woman.

"Excuse me," said Scott, looking at the woman's upraised eyebrows and open mouth. "I'm just . . . just . . . going out the back door to get some Coke for Jackson."

The woman pressed a hand to her chest and leaned against the wall. "Thank goodness," she breathed. "I thought you might be one of those protestors gotten loose inside. Now, excuse me, but I've got to get this fellow into bed." She reached for the trolley and for the first time Scott looked at what lay on the table.

Although it was covered with a sheet and its head was pointing away from hm, the size indicated a dog, Scott decided. Except for the gentle up and down movement of the white sheet as the animal breathed, it lay still.

Scott stepped to one side to let the trolley pass.

"Sorry I scared you," he said. At that moment there was a quiet thump at the end of the cart as though the dog had tried to wag its tail. Then, as the woman nodded and began to push the cart past Scott, he saw that one of the dog's floppy ears was flipped up, exposing the pink inside.

Without thinking, Scott reached up and gently lowered the ear as the dog went by, smoothing it over the side of the dog's honey-gold head—Casey's head.

Chapter Eleven

Scott dashed blindly away from the cart and stumbled toward the door with the red exit sign above it. Outside, he clung to the blue railing at the top of the steps and tried to fill his lungs with air, but his chest was heaving as though he'd run a mile in six minutes and he couldn't seem to get it to stop.

Then suddenly he had to go to the bathroom worse than he'd ever had to go in his life. Frantic, he dashed across the lawn and into the small grove of trees on the far side, where he peed behind the largest eucalyptus.

Scott's breathing had settled by that time and he forced himself to walk to the store, buy a gigantic bottle of Coke, and walk back toward the lab, his head busy with thoughts.

Why didn't I hear Casey last night? What am I going to do? Maybe he was drugged. What am I going to do? Casey looked so sick. What are they doing to him in there? *What am I going to do?*

Scott climbed the steps to the back door and pressed on the thumb pad of the door handle. Locked, of course. He was about to go around to the front, where Jackson could let him in, no longer caring about the protestors, when he realized he'd be able to see Casey again if he went in the back. He'd be able to find out where he was. Maybe make a plan.

Scott banged on the back door. In a short while, the door opened a crack and one eyeball peered through. "I thought it was you," said the woman who had been wheeling Casey back to his cage. "Back with the Coke for our resident Coke-oholic." She opened the door wide enough for Scott to squeeze past.

"Thanks," he muttered, wishing he were brave enough to ask her what they'd done to Casey.

"I need to mention," the woman said as she closed the door behind Scott, "that you should never touch one of the research subjects without receiving permission first. That dog you touched has to be kept sterile. He's at a critical stage in an experiment right now and is very vulnerable. The wrong germs could ruin everything."

"Sorry," Scott mumbled, moving around her. He headed back toward the rodent room, certain that if he could figure out what the woman had just said, he'd learn something about what they were doing to Casey.

When Scott came to the door of the dog room, he took another quick peek around, then slipped inside.

Casey wasn't in any of the cages on the far wall. Scott remembered the woman saying Casey had to be kept sterile, so he decided he was probably in one of the cubicles. He looked in the one beside the retriever's. Empty. Holding his breath, he moved to the next cubicle. Pay dirt.

Scott opened the door and knelt beside the cage, the Coke bottle on the floor beside him. Casey looked as though he was still asleep, but when Scott poked his fingers through the cage wire and touched his nose, the dog lifted his head, and his tongue came out to flap weakly at the air beneath Scott's fingers.

"Casey," Scott whispered. "Oh, Casey." He squeezed his eyes shut so tight they watered, hoping when he opened them Casey would vanish like a ghoul in a bad dream. But, of course, he didn't. "Don't worry," he said, his hands clenched knuckle white around the cage wires. "I'll get you out. No matter what I have to do, I'll get you out of here."

He was tempted to scoop Casey into his arms and make a dash for it out the back door. But if he and Casey disappeared at the same time, he might as well have pinned a sign to his chest that morning that read, I'M GOING TO STEAL A DOG FROM THE LAB TODAY. The police would be on his doorstep before he even made it home. No, rescuing Casey had to be planned properly. He didn't want anything to go wrong.

Scott gave Casey's muzzle a soft finger stroke, grabbed the Coke, then closed the door to the cubicle and headed toward the rodent room, memorizing every step of the way. He pushed the bar that opened the door and realized it was a door that locked automatically on one side only—the other side.

While Scott fed and watered his charges, his mind was frantically trying to think of a way to rescue Casey. For certain he'd tell his parents when he got home. But then, with Dr. Wilder out of town, they might not be able to do anything anyway. And once they knew about Casey, Scott wouldn't be able to do anything as crazy as stealing Casey out of the lab, because it would be obvious who was guilty. So telling his parents definitely limited his options. In which case, he'd need a way into the lab. He'd need keys.

74

He knew there was no way he could get Jackson's keys off him. Usually a place like this had a second set of keys -hanging around somewhere, though. Maybe in Jackson's office. If he could search it, he might luck out. But first he had to get rid of Jackson.

I think I know how to do that, Scott told himself. I just have to be patient.

He knew Jackson's habits, knew that sooner or later all that pop he drank would catch up to him and he'd have to go to the toilet. The rest room was just across the rodent room, so it wouldn't give Scott enough time to explore the office, but it would give him enough time to put a plan into action.

Finally Jackson headed for the rest room. As soon as the door swung shut behind him, Scott raced for the cubicle. He grabbed Jackson's bottle of Coke and ran with it toward the sink behind the last row of cages. Quickly he dumped most of it down the drain, leaving only a bit in the bottom. He ran back to the cubicle, slammed the bottle down on the desk and made it to the nearest cage before Jackson shoved through the rest room door. Now it would be only a matter of minutes.

It took less than that.

"What the . . .?" he heard Jackson mutter almost immediately. "What happened to my Coke?"

He stomped out of his office and over to Scott. "You drank my Coke," he accused, his brow creased and his eyebrows bunched.

"No, sir," said Scott. "I didn't."

"Then what happened to it? It didn't just evaporate into the air."

Scott opened his eyes wide and tried to look innocent. "Sometimes when I'm busy thinking about something, I can eat a whole bag of M&Ms without even knowing it," he said.

"Are you suggesting I'm so spaced out I drank it all in twenty minutes and didn't even know it?"

Scott shrugged.

"Breathe on me!"

"Huh?" Jackson's demand caught him by surprise.

"I said, breathe on me. If you didn't drink it you don't have anything to hide, right?"

"Right," Scott muttered, taking a step backward. If guilt or innocence could be detected by the thudding of his heart, however, he was certain Jackson would know what he'd done if he'd just shut up and listen. Lucky for Scott, he didn't.

"So, breathe!" Jackson ordered again.

Scott leaned forward and blew in Jackson's face, wishing he'd had a raw garlic and onion sandwich for lunch.

Jackson shook his head. "So maybe we have a ghost."

Scott now *held* his breath, knowing what Jackson did next would determine whether or not Scott got to search the office. If Jackson headed back into his office, Scott had guessed wrong and he would lose his chance. If not . . .

Jackson reached into his pants pocket and Scott let out his breath. With the rest of the day again looming ahead of him without his bottle to suck on, Jackson was going to ask Scott to go for more.

But Scott was prepared. "Here," Jackson said, handing Scott some more money. "Go buy me another bottle." He shook his head the way Scott's father did when he was trying to remember a name he'd forgotten. "Maybe I'll remember drinking this one," he said.

"I can't," Scott said. Then, as though the faster the speech, the less deceitful the lie, he added, "I have a dentist's appointment at three. If I go to the store again, I won't be done with the feeding early enough to get to my appointment on time."

Jackson swore under his breath, then rammed the money into his pocket. "I'll go myself," he muttered. He glanced toward the door leading to the hallway and the back door exit, as though he might consider walking to the store. Then he shrugged, dug his car keys out of his pocket, and headed toward the front door and the parking lot. In a few seconds, he'd pushed through the doorway and Scott was alone.

Chapter Twelve

Alone! Scott had ten, maybe fifteen minutes before Jackson got back. He turned and ran to Jackson's cubicle. Not daring to make a mess, he carefully opened drawers and peered under piles of papers. No keys. Scott glanced at his watch. Jackson had been gone four minutes. Scott had time to do a more thorough search if he were careful not to disturb anything and give himself away. He was starting to look in a cupboard beside the door when the outside door opened and Jackson appeared.

Scott actually felt his stomach drop, as though it had simply plunged to the bottom of his abdomen in a hole left by his unexpectedly absent guts.

His first instinct was to fall to the floor and hope Jackson headed first to the rest room, giving him time to sneak out of the office. He was glad he ignored that instinct when he saw that Jackson had his back turned and was staring out at the parking lot. Quickly Scott darted around the corner and down a row of cages.

He took a deep breath before asking, "What's going on?" Nevertheless his voice squeaked.

Jackson didn't seem to notice. He was too busy peering out the door. "Couldn't get out of the parking lot," he said. "Arf blocked my car."

Scott hurried over and peeked around Jackson's shoulder. The members of A.R.F. stood in a line, their arms linked. The dog with the Gandhi sign was barking. The one that had been rescued from an experiment was cowering under its owner's feet.

Facing them was a line of F.I.F.A.R. members, also with linked arms. A couple of people on both sides were shouting through bullhorns. The rest were just shouting. Between the bellowing and the barking Scott couldn't understand a word either side said. The only person keeping his mouth shut was Peter. Probably because a policeman was shaking a nightstick in his face.

"Bunch of crazies," Jackson muttered. "Next thing you know, one of those Arf nuts will take it into his head to plant a bomb or something."

Scott started to protest that remark, but decided he might be wiser to keep his opinions to himself. Instead, he said, "I heard that those organizations sometimes break into labs and free the animals."

Jackson snorted. "Yeah, I guess we should be happy we're dealing with Arf and not one of those other weirdo groups. Arf makes a lot of noise, but hasn't done anything illegal."

"Well, you never know," Scott answered, his mouth dry. He'd done it. He'd planted the seed. He didn't like doing it, but if he were going to save Casey, he had to take drastic measures. Because now, A.R.F. would get blamed when he, Scott Richmond, broke into the lab. Because, unless he found a key, that was what he'd have to do.

79

Jackson glanced at his watch. "Only two-ten," he groaned. "Guess I'll have to go to the store the back way."

Scott felt a flare of hope at his words. Another chance. "Two-ten?" he asked, trying to sound surprised. "I'd better get busy or I'll be late for my dentist appointment."

After the hall door clicked shut behind Jackson, Scott went back to the cupboard he'd started to search when Jackson came back so unexpectedly. There was nothing there, but as he closed the cupboard, he noticed a shallow metal cabinet hanging on the back of the office door. He'd never seen it before because the door was always open, so the cabinet was hidden against the wall.

Scott swung the office door partly closed and took a better look. The cabinet door had a knob and a lock on it. He turned the knob and the door swung open. Scott heaved a sigh. The cabinet was full of hooks with keys hanging on them. Each hook had a location written above it that matched its key, which had a round, white paper tag attached with the location written on it.

"Office Supplies," Scott read. "Cleaning Supplies. Medical Equipment. Furnace Room." The names continued, all of them for doors Scott didn't give a hoot about. Then he saw a hook labelled Hall Doors, and knew it was a copy of the one Jackson had used. He lifted the key off the hook and pocketed it.

Now all I need is one to the outside doors, he told himself, scanning the remaining hooks. Then he saw it. Master Key, he read. Master key—the key that would open any door in the building. It was all he would need. But Scott felt like a balloon that had just been pricked. The master-key hook was empty.

After a quick search of the other tags, in case the master key had accidentally been put on the wrong hook, Scott gave up and closed the cabinet door. There was no key on the board that would let him into the building. He'd have to find another way, perhaps a vent or a window to crawl through or . . .

Or what? he asked himself. Or what? His shoulders sagged. It was hopeless. Without a key, he'd have to break in for sure. And he didn't know if he had the guts to do that. Then he thought about Casey lying in the cage down the hall and he fingered the hall key hidden in his pocket and went to finish his job.

When Scott stepped out the door of the lab a while later, he took one look toward his bike and decided to leave it there. On the sidewalk in front of the office area, A.R.F. was marching in a ragged circle, chanting. In the parking lot a few feet away, F.I.F.A.R. was marching in another ragged circle, chanting. The bike rack was in between. A couple of police officers were standing off to one side of the parking lot.

Even with the police there Scott didn't feel like getting between the two groups of protestors. He'd walk home. It would give him time to think.

By the time Scott reached home he felt lousier than ever. The thought of breaking into the lab made his stomach hurt. The only thing to do was to tell his parents and hope they'd be able to help, even though Dr. Wilder was out of town, he decided, as he unlocked the door and called for his mother. Silence told Scott his mother and Julie still weren't home from the doctor's. I guess Julie feels better so they went shopping, he decided.

Scott was planning the speech he'd use to tell his parents about Casey when his father's car screeched to a stop in the driveway, and, seconds later, Mr. Richmond slammed through the door and raced up the stairs.

"Scott!" he hollered as he ran. "Scott! Come here. Quick."

Scott had never heard his father sound the way he did, as though a hole had suddenly opened up in the ground in front of him and he had nearly fallen in. "Coming," he called, and took the stairs two at a time.

His father had a suitcase on the bed and was throwing clothes into it, helter-skelter. "Find the little white suitcase Julie uses when we go on vacation," he ordered. "Put in some of her pajamas, her bathrobe, slippers, and some of her favorite books and games."

"What's going on?" Scott asked.

"Just do as I say!" his dad barked, not even looking up from his packing.

It was the first time Scott could ever remember his father yelling at him for no reason. He was so shocked, he couldn't move, just kept standing in the doorway, staring at his frantic father.

"Scott, move!" his father shouted again.

Scott's eyes started to sting and he got a thick, heavy feeling behind his eyebrows. First, he finds Casey at the lab. Then his father turns into a bellowing bully for no reason. It was too much. "What's going on?" he whispered, his voice wavering.

His dad looked up. "Didn't you get your mother's phone call?" he asked.

82

Scott shook his head. "I just got home."

Suddenly, Mr. Richmond's body seemed to lose all its bones and he sank onto the bed, looking shriveled and old. "Scott, I'm sorry," he said. He patted the bed. "Come here and sit. There's something I have to tell you." His dad paused to take a deep breath. "Julie might be sicker than we thought," he said then. "Your mother has taken her to U.C.L.A. Medical Center for some tests. I'm going to meet them there. We'll probably spend the night. There's also a chance Julie might have to stay in the hospital for a while." He ran his fingers wearily through his hair. "I don't think you should come to the hospital now. I want you to stay with Tim tonight. I'll come home tomorrow no matter what."

"But what's the matter with Julie anyway? It's not anything serious, is it? It can't be anything serious." Scott's voice sounded tight, even to his own ears, as though his vocal cords had suddenly been stretched, like the strings on a guitar when the musician tightens the tuning pegs.

"We don't know yet," his father said. "That's why she has to have the tests. It could be something as simple as some type of anemia. That means her body doesn't have enough of the stuff it needs to make red blood cells. And that can be fixed. Or . . . or it could be something like . . . like leukemia."

Leukemia! Scott didn't know much about leukemia. All he knew was that in the second grade Cheryl Timchuk had announced in show-and-tell that her cousin had leukemia. A few months later, Cheryl said her cousin had died.

"Leukemia?" Scott said then. "But . . . but . . . when kids get that they . . . they . . . die."

"No!" his father shouted, as though Scott had said a word so terrible even the saying of it could kill. "No, they don't! Not anymore. The doctor said there are different kinds. If it is leukemia—and I know it's not—it can be cured, unless maybe it's a real, real bad kind. But Julie doesn't have leukemia. I'd know if she had leukemia. And she doesn't. I know she doesn't."

"But what is it—exactly?" Scott asked. "Leukemia."

Scott's father shook his head. "I'm not sure how to explain it. Somehow the body stops making healthy blood. Some people call it cancer of the blood, but it's not. Not really. It's more like cancer of the tissues that make blood cells. At least that's what your mother said the doctor said. But she also said to not even think the word leukemia. It's probably just anemia." At that moment Scott's father did something else Scott had never seen him do. His face folded up, then he buried his head in his hands. "I *know* it's just anemia," he said, and began to sob.

Scott sat unmoving, as though turned to stone. At last he reached out and awkwardly patted his father's knee. "I know you're right," he whispered. "Julie doesn't have leukemia. It's probably just anemia."

But his father continued to sob, so Scott quietly got up and went off to pack Julie's suitcase.

Chapter Thirteen

A short time later Mr. Richmond was throwing the suitcases into the car.

"Here," said Scott, handing his father Julie's favorite doll. "We almost forgot Patty Cake."

"That would have been a disaster. I'd have had to turn right around and come back for it," said his dad, not looking at Scott. Instead, he stared at the doll's nearly bald head, then shook his own head. "I hate to leave you alone like this," he said, "but I don't think the hospital is the place for you right now." He turned and put his empty hand on Scott's shoulder. "Are you sure you'll be okay?" he asked, his red-rimmed eyes finally meeting Scott's. "I know you're worried about Julie and I don't like the thought of you not having any family around during a time like this."

Scott forced a smile. "Tim's like family," he said, hoping this would make his father feel better about leaving him.

"You phone him right away," his dad ordered. "Explain things to him and make certain you can spend the night. I don't want to have to worry about you, too. As soon as I get to the hospital, I'll phone Mrs.

Wilder and leave the number where we can be reached."

Scott nodded, then suddenly found himself crushed against his father's chest. It had been a while since his father had done more than throw an arm around Scott's shoulders, slap him on the back, or pat his cheek, so for a second Scott felt uncomfortable. Then he wanted to snuggle right in, burst into tears, and let his father know how truly frightened and worried he was, how all he wanted right then was to be with his parents and Julie, not left on his own like some grown-up kid. But he stopped the sobs before they started, and gave his father a hug.

"I love you, Scott," said his dad, before turning to climb into the car and back down the driveway. Leaving to go to Julie. Leaving Scott on his own.

It wasn't until his father's car had disappeared down the street that Scott realized he hadn't told him about Casey.

All his life Scott had heard the expression, "That was the straw that broke the camel's back." And now, for the first time, he thought he understood it. Between Casey and Julie, in one day he'd been loaded with more worries than he could handle. Now suddenly he had to carry them on his own. But it wasn't only worries that weighed him down, he realized. It was guilt.

Scott remembered how he ignored Julie whenever she signed "I love you," and the thought hit him like a punch in the gut. He remembered how much he resented her, how ticked he felt whenever she got her own way, how he called her Ghoul Jule in secret, but Cool Jule to her face.

Scott made it into the house before the tears broke.

He was still sitting on the sofa, sobbing, when he heard a knock at the door.

He ignored it, hoping whoever it was would leave, then heard a second knock. Scott swiped at his eyes with the back of his hand and went to the door. He stood on tiptoes and peered through the peephole. There was an eyeball on the other side looking in. Scott jumped back, even though he knew no one could see in from that side. Cautiously he put his eye to the hole again. This time he saw Cristina, looking head swollen and body shrunken, as the peephole always made people appear.

Cripes! Scott thought. Cristina Martinez is the last person I want to see right now. He scrubbed at his eyes and cheeks again. If she knows I've been crying, she'll think I'm a real weenie, Scott told himself as he opened the door.

If Cristina noticed Scott had been crying, she didn't mention it. She just narrowed her dark eyes slightly and said, *"Tia* told me where you live, so I came to see if you went to the pound this morning. You said last night you were going to try again."

Scott nodded. "Yeah. No luck."

"Well, I guess whoever took Casey likes him," Cristina suggested, bobbing up on her toes and peering over Scott's shoulder. "You get in okay last night?" she asked.

"No problem."

"You alone?"

"Yeah."

"You got anything to drink? I'm dry."

"Come on in," he said, not wanting company, but knowing what she meant by being dry. Suddenly he couldn't have worked up enough spit to wet a stamp.

Scott was just closing the door behind Cristina when he heard Tim call out, "Hold it, Muttman." Tim thumped up the steps and stuck his head in the door. His eyeglasses slipped an inch when he saw Cristina standing behind Scott. "Hey, man. What's going on?" He shoved his glasses back up his nose.

Scott opened the door and pulled Tim inside. "Boy, am I glad to see you," he mouthed to Tim. Then he pointed over his shoulder and said in a louder voice, "This is Cristina Martinez. She's spending the summer with Mrs. Sanchez, her aunt—I mean her great-aunt. She came over to ask if I'd checked the pound for Casey this morning."

Cristina gave a little wave in Tim's direction.

Scott shoved Tim toward Cristina. "This is my best friend, Tim Wilder."

"I sort of gathered that—Muttman," Cristina said, looking as though she wanted to laugh.

"Cristina wanted something to drink," Scott explained. "You want something too—*don't* you?" he added, pushing Tim ahead of him toward the kitchen.

"Sure, I guess," Tim said. "As long as you're not stingy with the ice this time."

When the three of them had their drinks, they sat around the kitchen table, silently staring into their glasses as though some fascinating play were being acted out under the ice cubes. Scott squirmed, trying hard to think of something brilliant to say. Instead, he cracked his knuckles.

Both Tim and Cristina glared at him. "There are quite a few gross noises in the world," Cristina said. "But I happen to think knuckle-cracking is one of the grossest."

"Absolutely," agreed Tim.

"Sooor-r-r-y," Scott said. He tried to sound smooth, but his voice cracked as loudly as his knuckles had. He'd been through enough for one day. He didn't need some dumb girl telling him he was gross. He felt Cristina's eyes boring into him and looked down at his drink. Just in time, because he could feel his eyes burn and tears start to well up again. Not now, he pleaded silently. Please, not now.

Suddenly, out of the blue, Cristina said, "You've been crying."

Scott wanted to crawl under the table, curl into a ball, and evaporate. Instead, he raised his head and looked her right in the eye. "I have not," he said.

"Have too," Cristina snapped. "Reporters learn to notice details like that. It makes better copy."

"Then you'll make a lousy reporter, because I have not." But even as he spoke, one lone tear slipped out of Scott's eye and slid down his cheek.

"You're still worried about Casey, aren't you?" Tim asked, plunking his drink down onto the table.

How humiliating, Scott thought, crying in front of a girl. He swiped at his eyes as he shook his head no. Then he nodded his head yes.

"So which is it? Yes or no?"

"It's both. It's neither. It's awful," Scott said, wondering where to start. Then he decided to start with Julie.

"Julie . . ." He looked at Cristina and added, "She's my little sister. Julie's sick." He went on to tell Cristina and Tim everything his father had told him.

"Jeez," Tim said when he finished. "Jeez. That's . . . that's rotten."

"Yeah," agreed Scott.

Tim leaned forward. "But even if it is, you know,

leukemia, Julie will beat it. You know she will. She's a tough little kid. Remember that time she fell on the gravel and scraped her knees practically down to the bone. She screeched bloody murder when your mom had to pick out all the dirt and bits of rock, but she healed real fast."

Scott nodded. He sat up straighter. "And then there was the time she fell off her riding car and split her lip open. She healed fast that time, too."

"And she got right back on the car again, didn't she?" Tim asked. "See, she's a fighter. She'll be okay."

"Yeah," said Scott. "She'll be okay. There's probably nothing serious wrong anyway. And even if there is, she'll be okay."

Cristina, who'd been silent, added quietly, "If Julie's anything like her brother, I *know* she'll be fine."

Tim raised his eyebrows.

No doubt he's wondering how Cristina knows me well enough to say that, Scott thought. I wish I'd told Tim about Cristina this morning. Now he'll think I've been trying to keep her a secret and he'll go and make a big deal out of it.

So what? he asked himself. There's more to worry about than getting teased by Tim. He hadn't even told them about Casey yet.

"But this stuff about Julie's not everything," he said then, feeling his throat thicken again and the tears threaten. "Casey wasn't adopted like we thought. He's—" Scott hesitated, wondering whether he should continue. He got up and went to the fridge for more pop, giving himself time to think.

It was okay to tell Cristina Casey was at the lab, but he wasn't so sure about Tim. Tim wasn't even supposed to learn about their midnight visit to I.B.L. And what if Tim's mother had told him Dr. Wilder was doing something wonderful? What if Tim believed animals *should* be used for research? It was, after all, his uncle and his uncle's lab.

"Casey's what? He's what?" Cristina asked, rattling her ice cubes impatiently, but shaking her head when Scott offered her more pop.

"Did you ask your mom about the kind of stuff your uncle does at the lab?" he asked Tim, stalling.

"No, I haven't seen her yet." Tim held up his glass to let Scott know he wanted more to drink.

Feeling better, Scott filled Tim's glass. If Tim hadn't talked to his mother, he wouldn't know any more than he had learned from reading the paper at Scott's that morning. "Casey's at the lab," he said quickly, before stopping to think about it. "I think he's being used in an experiment."

Cristina choked on the ice cube she'd been sucking and spit it back into her glass.

Tim's mouth fell open and his eyes grew wide behind their blue-tinted lenses. "No way!" he exclaimed. He was quiet for a second, then he threw back his head and slapped the table. "I get it," he said with a laugh. "You joined this A.R.F. thing and now you want me to join too. It would look real good for the group if Dr. Wilder's nephew picketed the place. So you think that by telling me Casey is in the lab I'll get mad enough to demonstrate with you." He sat back in his chair and grinned at Scott. "That's it, isn't it?" he asked.

Scott shook his head. "I wish it was, but Casey is really, truly in the lab. I saw him this morning." He

91

went on to tell Tim and Cristina about how he had seen Casey on the trolley and later in his cage.

When Scott finished, he decided both of them looked as though a vampire had sucked out all their blood. For a minute neither said anything, just looked at Scott with their eyes scrinched. Then Cristina said, "So what are we going to do about it?"

"I was going to tell my parents and see if they could help. Maybe phone Dr. Wilder or something. But then this thing with Julie came up and . . ."

"And my uncle's out of town anyway," Tim finished.

Scott nodded. "What about your parents?" he asked Tim. "Could they do anything?"

"Maybe. They talked to my uncle on the phone last night. About the protestors I guess. I suppose they could phone him and tell him about Casey. Then my uncle could phone the lab and tell them to let you take Casey. Then . . ." Tim paused. "Then the lab would tell my uncle that they'd already started doing tests on Casey and—"

"And your uncle would say 'Forget it,' " Scott added.

Tim nodded. "I've heard my parents talking about how important my uncle's research is. If they knew Casey was already being used for tests, I doubt they'd even phone him. And even if they did, for certain my uncle wouldn't let Casey go if he's already part of some experiment."

"So it's up to me," Scott muttered.

"So it's up to *us,*" Cristina corrected.

"Right," Tim agreed. "Now what are *we* going to do?"

"You sure you want in on this?" Scott asked Tim.

92

"I wasn't sure I should even tell you, since it's your uncle's lab and all."

Tim nodded. "I want in."

"Okay, you're in." Scott pulled the hall key out of his pocket and showed it to Tim and Cristina. "I have the key that opens the hall doors. I'm going to try to get into the lab tonight and sneak Casey out, but I haven't figured out how to get inside yet. I guess we'll have to find a way to break in."

We'll have to find a way. The words sounded wonderful to Scott. *We'll* have to find a way. No longer was it only Scott, or even Scott and Cristina. Now it was Scott and Cristina and Tim. He had help. The thought almost made him cry again.

"Breaking in would be a real dumb thing to do," Tim said. "A real dumb thing to do, especially since I have—a key."

"What?!" Scott screeched. "You have a key? Give it to me. Let me see it."

"I don't have it on me, Jell-O brain. It's at home. My dad's the insurance agent for my uncle, so my parents always have a key to the lab—in case anything happens while my uncle's out of town and Dad needs to get into the building when it's closed."

"The key, can you get it?" Scott asked, cracking his knuckles, finger by finger.

"I think so. It's in the pantry. I hope I can remember what it looks like because it doesn't have a tag on it or anything. Just in case someone breaks into our house and steals it, my parents don't want the jerky thief to know what it's for."

"How soon can you get it?" Cristina asked, reaching out to smack Scott on the back of one hand to get him to stop cracking.

93

"Anytime, I suppose." He looked at Scott. "Before dinner if you want. What time are you planning to use it?"

Scott made a face. "Late, I guess. During the night." He groaned. "I almost forgot. I'm supposed to stay at your house tonight."

"That'd wreck everything," said Tim. "We couldn't sneak out."

"We need a plan," Cristina suggested.

"I guess we do," Tim agreed. "Let's get to work."

The three of them spent the next hour on their plan to rescue Casey. It gave Scott the shivers just thinking about actually doing any of it, but he decided it would be a pretty good plan—after a few changes he'd announce at the right time.

"So let's head over to my house," Tim said finally. "Mom should be getting home about now. I'd like to find that key before she gets there."

"And my dad'll be phoning your house from the hospital soon," said Scott. "We've got to be there before he does."

"I'll meet you at eleven then," Cristina said as they pushed themselves away from the table. "Remember, you left your bike at the lab," she added, shaking her finger at Scott, "so it'll take longer to get there tonight. Don't fall asleep and be late again."

"What did she mean 'late *again*'?" Tim asked, after Scott had locked the house and Cristina had disappeared toward Mrs. Sanchez's. Tim's bike wobbled crazily as he tried to ride slowly enough for Scott to keep up on foot.

"I suppose I better tell you everything," Scott said, "or you'll bug me until we're old enough to be fossils."

94

When Scott finished telling Tim about his midnight visit to the lab with Cristina the night before, about hiding from the guard, about not hearing Casey, Tim said, "I'm kinda ticked at you for not letting me in on all this last night, but I suppose I'll forgive you. I'm just glad this Cristina is only here for the summer. Otherwise, I'd have to start looking for a girlfriend, too, so we'd still have something to talk about. Tell me, does she kiss nice?"

Scott started to splutter, and made a fist to punch Tim in the arm, then realized his friend was teasing. "Kiss her?!" he asked, his voice rising. "Kiss her? I have enough trouble *talking* to her."

As the boys walked and wobbled their way down the street, Scott felt better. Perhaps it was because of Tim's teasing. Perhaps it was because someone was sharing his load with him. Or maybe he felt better because he was actually doing something about part of that load. He wished he could be doing something for Julie, to make sure she was okay, to make himself feel better about the way he'd often treated her. But he couldn't change the past; he could only make it up to Julie in the future. He just hoped she had a future. In the meantime, he was glad he could do something for Casey. At least he'd try.

Chapter Fourteen

Tim and Scott were in the Wilders' kitchen pantry sorting through the keys in an old cookie tin, when they heard Mrs. Wilder come through the garage door.

"Not enough time," Tim hissed, grabbing some keys and shoving the rest at Scott. Quickly the boys crammed them into their pockets.

"Remember, don't mention anything about Julie being sick or my parents being in Los Angeles," Scott reminded Tim just before Mrs. Wilder poked her head around the pantry door.

"Caught you!" she said with a laugh, cradling a bag of groceries in her arms. "Don't you dare eat anything. Supper is in a half hour, or in an hour, or maybe in an hour and a half. It all depends on how quickly this poor, exhausted, overworked person can get organized." She heaved a dramatic sigh and batted her eyelashes. Then she grinned a goofy grin and added, "But mostly it depends on whether or not you'll set the table." She poked her head farther in the door. "Oh, hi, Scott. I didn't see you there behind the water jug."

"Hi, Mrs. Wilder," said Scott.

"Hi, Mom," said Tim. "I invited Scott for dinner. That okay?"

"As long as he still likes spaghetti."

"He still loves it," said Tim, as his mother disappeared around the pantry door.

"I love it," echoed Scott. "Thanks."

In a second they heard paper and plastic rustle as Mrs. Wilder started to unpack the groceries.

"Come on," whispered Tim. "Let's go to my room and sort through these keys."

"Don't forget we have to stay near the phone," said Scott. "We don't want your mother answering it."

"Right," agreed Tim as the two boys headed toward the stairs, their right hands shoved into their pockets to hide any key bulge. "We'll take the upstairs hall phone into my bedroom."

"About *face!*" called Mrs. Wilder, just as they made it to the bottom step. "You're going to set the table, remember?"

"In a minute, Mom."

"N-o-o-ow. I'm going to change my clothes. I want to see the table set when I come back."

Tim sighed and the boys headed back toward the kitchen. They finished setting the table just as Mrs. Wilder reappeared.

"We're outta here," Tim muttered, again heading for his bedroom. At that moment the phone rang.

"I'll get it!" Tim yelled, nearly flattening his mother as he raced past her to the kitchen phone.

"Yeah, everything's fine," he said a second later. "No problem. She's right here. Yeah, she knows. Yeah, he's right here, too." He lowered the phone. "It's your dad," he told Scott, his face as blank as a Ken doll's face.

97

"He wants to talk to you. You can use the phone in the family room.

"Mr. Richmond just wanted to make sure it's okay for Scott to stay for dinner," Scott heard Tim tell his mother as Scott headed for the family room. "He was worried that I hadn't asked you first."

Scott's hand shook as he reached for the phone. He stared at the hand as though he had never seen that particular one before. For sure, he'd never seen it shake before. Why? he wondered. Because of news his father might have about Julie? Or because the plan to rescue Casey was now set in motion and the slightest slipup could wreck it?

"Hi, Dad," he said, his voice quivering.

"Everything okay?" his father asked.

"Yeah. Fine. How's Julie?"

"They're doing a bone marrow test on her now. I'll let you know in the morning how things are going. Got a pencil? I want to give you the number here in case you need to reach us. Then let me talk to Tim's mom."

"No!" said Scott, too loud even to his own ears. "I mean, you can't. 'Cuz she isn't here."

"Tim just finished telling me she was."

"She is. I mean she was. But while I was coming to the phone I heard her tell Tim she was going next door for something."

"Okay," said his father. "Just be sure to give her the number here. She should have it."

"I will," agreed Scott, his stomach rolling over as the lies started to pile up.

When Scott hung up the phone, he shoved the slip of paper with the phone number into his pocket and went back to the kitchen. He was about to tell another lie. He wondered if this one would seem easier.

"That was my dad," he said, as though Tim and his mother didn't already know. He opened his eyes wider so he'd look as innocent as possible, then added, "He said it's only fair that if you have to put up with me for dinner, my family should have to put up with Tim for the rest of the evening. He said it would be okay if Tim slept over at my house tonight. If it's okay with you, that is."

Mrs. Wilder opened her mouth in a wide circle. "What?" she asked. "Part with my precious son for an entire night?" She reached out, gently grabbed a fistful of Tim's black hair, and tugged him toward her. "I don't know," she said. "I don't know if I can bear to be away from him for that long."

Tim turned a shade darker than usual. "Oh, come off it, Mom," he mumbled, rolling his eyes.

"Well," she said, "then go. Go, though my heart is shattered by your fickle behavior." She shoved Tim away and threw an arm over her face.

"Getting in practice for tryouts next week?" Tim asked, poking at his glasses. His mother loved acting and was a member of an amateur theater group.

"Yeah, how was I?"

Tim squeezed his nose shut. "Peee-ew!"

"That bad, huh? Oh, well. Go get your brother, will you? I saw him next door at Jeremy's when I came home."

"Don't you two stay up all night," Tim's dad told the boys later, as they left for Scott's. "On second thought," he added, "go ahead. That way you won't need to try it when you're both sleeping here, and you

99

can drive Scott's parents nuts instead of us." He laughed as he shut the door behind them.

"I'm glad we still have to run the dogs," Scott told Tim. "It'll kill some time."

"Lead on, Muttman," said Tim. "We've got a lot of time to kill."

"Only eight o'clock," he groaned an hour later when they reached Scott's house. "We should have given the dogs a walk, not a run."

The evening seemed to drag on forever. When the alarm clock finally went off at 10:30, Scott nearly squirted out of his skin.

"Jeez," complained Tim, who had also jumped when the alarm buzzed, "I know you were afraid you'd fall asleep and be late again, but you could have warned me that thing sounds like a fire alarm."

"Sorry. You know what a heavy sleeper I am. I need a loud alarm to wake me in the morning."

"That would wake a vampire in the daytime," Tim said.

"Aw, quit complaining and let's go," Scott ordered. "I'll just be glad when this is all over." He paused, then asked, "Have you thought about what you're going to do if we get caught?"

"I'm going to plead insanity," Tim replied.

"Good idea. It's the truth."

"If *I'm* insane, I wonder what that makes you?" Tim asked, and pushed Scott out the door.

It had been a cloudy day, and now it was a cloudy night. Not a single ray of moonlight or star twinkle broke through the overcast. "Perfect," said Tim. "No moon. Good and dark."

They got to the meeting place near the junior high

school early. A few minutes later Cristina appeared. She was completely dressed in black. Scott looked at the yellow sweatshirt he wore and the white tee shirt Tim had on and smacked himself on the forehead. Camouflage! Why hadn't he thought of that? He and Tim might as well have flashing neon tubes plastered all over them.

"Did you get the key?" Cristina asked.

There was a breath of silence. Then Tim said. "Of course we got the key. As a matter of fact, we got a whole—lot—of—keys." He rammed his hand into his pocket and pulled out the handful of keys he had shoved in it hours earlier.

"A—*whole*—lot—of—keys," Scott repeated, slowly opening his own hand to reveal another clutch of keys.

"We forgot to sort them," Tim groaned. "How could we have been so dumb?"

"You're boys, that's why," Cristina said.

Scott sent her a look that would have withered her in the daylight. But in the dark, it was wasted.

"So, what do we do?" Tim asked. "We don't dare stand under a streetlight to sort through them."

"No *problema,*" said Cristina, motioning them under a nearby pepper tree with low branches. With a flourish she pulled a penlight from her pocket and snapped it on.

Scott shook his head. First camouflage clothes, now a flashlight. The girl didn't miss a beat.

One by one Tim examined the keys they had brought.

"This one is too small. I think it's for a suitcase," he said. "This one's a skeleton key, so it must be for my house." Tim's house was at least seventy years

101

old and had a lot of old-fashioned doors and locks. "I think this is the extra key to my dad's car. I don't know what this one is. Maybe for a padlock. It's too small for a door key though." As he examined the keys, Tim divided them into Scott's and Cristina's palms. When he was finished, Cristina had about nine keys in her hand. Scott had four keys in his.

Tim poked a finger at Scott's bunch. "One of these has to be it," he explained. "They all look like door keys. But they're so much alike I can't tell which one belongs to the lab." He put Cristina's rejected keys back into his pocket and reached for Scott's four. "We'll just have to try them all," he said.

Scott closed his hand on the keys. *I'll* have to try them all. I'm the only one going into the lab. You guys are waiting outside."

"What?" Tim's and Cristina's angry screeches exploded into the darkness. "That's not the way we planned it," Cristina hissed.

"It sure isn't," said Tim, but Scott thought Tim sounded a bit relieved.

"I know," Scott said. "But I've been thinking about it. Tim can't go in. Not into his own uncle's lab."

"Well, it's not *my* uncle's lab," snapped Cristina. "I'm going in."

"No, you're not," said Scott. "If you get caught, they'll probably send you back home to Calexico. Then what would your *tia* do? You're supposed to be here to help her out. A lot of help you'd be back home. And then *your* family would be mad at *her* for not keeping a better eye on you."

Both Tim and Cristina were quiet for a minute. "And what's your excuse?" Cristina asked then. "I suppose nothing will happen to you if you get caught.

Like, I suppose you'll still be able to go to work there every day. And I suppose your family won't be mad at you 'cuz you're their little angel." If sarcasm were honey, Scott could have spread her words on toast.

"I've thought about that," Scott said. "My parents would be mad at me, but they're so worried about Julie right now, they won't have time to be mad for long. Tim can tell his uncle I learned about Casey and my sister on the same day and was so upset I didn't know what I was doing. No one would dare send me to Juvie Hall after a story like that."

"You've got it all figured out, haven't you?" Cristina fumed. "Well, you know what? I have more right to go into that lab than you do. You may work there, Mr. Bright Brain, but Casey is a member of *my* family. You're just his walker."

She was right. Scott had to admit it. Cristina was right. He sighed. "Okay," he said. "But if you get caught and sent home, don't blame me."

"So what do I do?" Tim asked. "I might as well have stayed home."

"Don't be stupid," Scott told him. "We needed the key—and we need a lookout."

"Okay. Okay. So let's do it." As Tim stood up and took off at a run, the gray clouds that had threatened all day finally unloaded.

"It's raining," panted Scott, catching up with Tim. "It never rains at this time of year."

"That's good," said Tim. "It'll cover our tracks."

"Not if it quits before we get there," Cristina said, puffing up behind them. "Then it'll just make nice fresh mud for us to *leave* tracks in."

Oh boy, thought Scott, as the threesome jogged toward I.B.L. Suddenly he wished they could simply disappear into a science fiction story where they could keep running on through the dark forever, without getting tired, without reaching their destination. Because suddenly he realized the seriousness of what they planned to do. Not only was it scary, it was against the law. His head warned him to reverse direction and go the other way, but his heart remembered Casey.

Chapter Fifteen

Soon the boxy, black bulk of I.B.L. squatted in the damp darkness ahead of them. A few moments later, they were hunched down behind the hawthorn bushes Cristina and Scott had hidden behind the night before.

"You wait here," Scott told Tim. "Once we're inside, whistle Casey's whistle if you see that guard coming. We're earlier tonight, so we should miss him, but just in case . . . When you whistle, we won't be able to hear you, but it'll set the dogs off and we'll hear them. Then we can hide. When the guard's gone and the dogs are quiet again, give a wolf whistle."

"What's a wolf whistle?" Cristina asked.

"You know. That's what guys whistle when they think a girl's cute."

"Oh, yeah. I just didn't know it was called a wolf whistle."

"Will you two quit yakking and get going," Tim ordered. "I don't get to come in out of the rain, remember. So just hurry it up." He hunched his back and tugged at the wet tee shirt plastered to his shoulders.

"We're outta here," Scott whispered and started

across the rain-wet lawn toward the building, Cristina close behind.

"Good luck," Tim called quietly after them.

Out of habit, Scott headed toward the door to the rodent room. At the corner of the building, he motioned Cristina to wait. "You stay here until I get the door open. Watch for that guard. Tim'll warn us once we're inside, but it's your job till then."

"Yes, *sir*," Cristina said in a voice that showed she didn't appreciate getting bossed around. "What'll I do if he comes? Yell, 'Cops!'?"

Scott bent and felt along the wall for a stone. "Here," he said. "If you see the car coming, pitch this at the concrete step. I'll hear it."

Cristina gave him a thumbs-up sign and squatted at the corner of the building under the eave, her back against the brick.

As Scott hurried to the entrance and up the steps, he checked to make sure his bike was still locked in the bike rack where he'd left it that afternoon. Then he pulled one key from his pocket. His hands were wet and cold from the rain and they shook as he tried to fit the key into the lock. At last he hit it. No go. He was about to try another key when Cristina's stone thunked against the concrete steps. Scott looked around to see a car turning into the parking lot. It moved slowly, its lights off, its engine scarcely a hum above the staccato of the rain. The rent-a-cop!

Scott's brain felt on fire, but his muscles were ice—frozen where he stood. By the time he had recovered his senses enough to run, it was too late. The car was pulling around to the front entrance. If the guard repeated last night's performance, he'd park beside the bike rack in front of the office. If Scott tried to run back to the corner of the building and across the lawn, the guard would see him for sure. He would have had a chance if he hadn't frozen—or if Cristina had kept a better watch and given an earlier warning—but now it was too late.

But it wasn't too late for his overheated brain to click into gear. If you can't retreat, attack, Scott told himself, jumping quickly off the steps and walking right toward the bike rack.

It'll work, he told himself. It'll work—as long as the guard didn't see me on the steps. I only hope Cristina has enough sense to get back around the corner and across the lawn to Tim while I have this guy's attention.

Scott strode up to the bike rack and opened the combination lock. He grabbed the handlebars just as the guard pulled up alongside and rolled down the passenger window. A bright beam of light flashed into Scott's eyes, blinding him.

"Out kinda late, aren't you, son?" the guard asked.

"Yes, sir," Scott replied, squinting into the light. "I work at the lab, and this afternoon when I left, all those protestors were marching around, and I was afraid to come over and get my bike. I was going to leave it here all night, but then it started to rain and I didn't want it to rust and . . ." His voice trailed off.

The guard cut the car's engine. "Why didn't your parents drive you over?"

Scott thought fast. "I . . . I didn't ask them. My sister's sick and they haven't been getting much sleep lately. So I . . . just . . . came myself."

The light snapped off, then the guard's door swung open and his boots clunked onto the pavement. He came around the car, and the closer he came, the bigger he seemed to grow. There was a small light above the building's main entrance, and when Scott's eyes readjusted to the dimness, he noticed the guard's bushy blond eyebrows that marched in a single line across his forehead. The single brow bunched up as he stared at Scott through the rain. From the lines on his face, Scott figured he was about as old as his grandparents, though maybe not quite. As the man loomed closer, Scott waited for the guard's gigantic hand to clamp down on his shoulder and haul him away. Instead, he felt his bike being dragged out from under his hands.

"Come on. I'll give you a ride home." The man wheeled Scott's bike to the back of the car and propped it against himself while he unlocked the trunk. "Darn protestors," he muttered. "I'll be glad when they all get on their way and let people attend to business."

Everything had happened so fast, Scott hadn't had time to react. Now a great, cold lump of fear rose up in him. All the warnings, all the horror stories he had ever heard rattled through his brain. No way! No way was he going to get into that car with that man. He didn't even know for certain the guy was a security guard. He might get in that car and never be heard from again. Forget Tim. Forget Cristina. Forget saving Casey. Scott had to save Scott.

Scott reached out and grabbed the bike's handlebars. "Thanks," he said, "but I'd rather just ride home."

"That's stupid," the guard said. "It's raining."

"I don't mind. I'd rather just ride home myself." His heart thumping, Scott tugged at the bike, but one pedal had caught under the edge of the bumper and it wouldn't budge. He let go of the bike and stepped back. If the man wouldn't give him the bike, Scott would leave it. It was better to lose a bike than to appear on one of those Missing Children milk cartons.

The guard got a puzzled look on his face. Then he shook his head. "I'm sorry," he said. "What was I thinking of? Kids don't get in cars with strangers. Not these days." He pushed the bike toward Scott. "Okay, you get now. I have to question and report anyone found on the grounds, but I won't tell if you won't tell."

Scott hopped onto the wet bicycle seat. "Thanks," he said.

"No problem. You did exactly what I taught my kids and grandkids to do. Sorry I scared you," he added, then called as Scott pedaled off, "Be careful. You don't have a light on that thing."

Scott raised an arm in reply as he splashed through a puddle and headed toward the dark lane leading away from I.B.L.

Chapter Sixteen

Scott pedaled so quickly down the lane, his tires spun on the slick pavement. When he was out of sight of the building, he jumped off the bike and wheeled it into the bushes. He squatted beside it until he heard the guard's car idle past, then he raced toward the shrubs where Tim—and he hoped Cristina—would be waiting.

They were. He crouched beside them and tried to catch his breath.

"Jeez!" exclaimed Tim. "I thought you were history for a minute there. I mean, I've never seen anything like that. You just walked up to that guy like you belonged here. I can't believe it! I can *not* believe it!"

"And I can't believe you," Scott said, giving Cristina a poke. "Some lookout you are. That car was practically on top of me before you saw it."

"Sorry," Cristina muttered, but she didn't look too upset. "The rain was pounding on that metal gutter above me and the car was quiet. No lights either."

"Well, I was hoping for a little more warning," said Scott.

"So, sue me."

"Forget it, both of you," Tim interrupted, flicking a drop of water off the end of his nose. "You're wasting time. If you don't get going, that guy will be back here on his next round—and I'll have pneumonia." As if to emphasize his words, he sneezed.

"What did you say to him, anyway?" Cristina asked. "We couldn't hear much."

"Never mind," said Tim. "He can tell us later." He reached out and gave Cristina and Scott a push.

"Last night, didn't you tell me there's a back door to this place?" Cristina asked as they stood up. By this time Scott's shoes were starting to squish and his clothes felt five pounds heavier.

Scott almost groaned out loud. What a bubble brain he was. Of course! He should have left Cristina at the front to watch, then gone to the back door. That way she could have crept back to warn him and they both would have had time to get away. It was only because he used the rodent room door every time he came and went that he had automatically gone to it earlier.

He nodded to Cristina and led the way across the lawn again, this time toward the back of the building.

The lock opened with the third key. Scott hesitated, wanting so badly to crack his knuckles he had to grab tightly to the door handle to keep them quiet. If he walked inside that door, he was breaking the law. Did he have the guts to do it? After all, it wasn't like he was rescuing a person or anything. Casey *was* only a dog.

"Move it!" Cristina, fed up with Scott taking so long, reached around him, pulled open the door, and gave him a shove. Whether or not he wanted to be, Scott was inside I.B.L.

111

He shivered. He didn't know whether it was from fear, from being wet and cold, or because the place seemed so eerie at night, lit only by the red exit light over the door.

A few dogs howled. That's better than total silence, Scott decided.

Scott motioned Cristina to follow him. They turned the corner of the hall, another exit light above the door to the rodent room giving them enough light to see where they were going. As they neared the dog room, Scott stopped. There—between dog howls—had he heard a cage rattle, or did he imagine it? He held his fingers to his lips and then cupped a hand around one ear to show Cristina what he was doing. There it was again. The rattle of a cage, as though the door had been opened and then shut again. It might have come from the room where the cats and monkeys were.

Goose bumps warted up all over Scott, and the hair on his arms rose. He took a step backward and tramped on Cristina's toe. He heard her suck in her breath, but other than that she didn't make a sound.

He was about to scurry back to the exit when four more rapid rattles staccatoed down the hall. At the same time a monkey screeched. Scott almost laughed out loud in relief. He cupped his hands around Cristina's ear and whispered, "It's probably just a monkey banging around in his cage. Maybe he's exercising."

Cristina put her hand over her heart and blew a puff of air to show how relieved she was.

Scott jerked his head in the direction of the dog room and Cristina nodded. Once again they started down the hall, silent step by silent step.

112

Dog smell attacked Scott's nose when they finally got into the room where he had seen Casey. Here, there was no light at all. Rain spattered against the windows, which looked gray against the blackness of the room.

Suddenly, a pinpoint of light pierced the darkness, glancing off the metal cages and off the white and red signs that declared the room a sterile area. Scott jumped, caught his breath, then remembered Cristina's penlight. He breathed again.

Scott pointed toward the cubicle where he'd seen Casey that afternoon. In a few steps he'd crossed the floor, opened the door, and was kneeling in front of the cage, hoping Casey was still here, hoping he was still alive. At that moment, the light glinted off the dog's honey-gold coat. Limp with relief, Scott slipped open the latch and reached in to touch the dog. Casey raised his head. His tail smacked weakly against the cage floor and he whimpered.

"Come on, boy," Scott coaxed. "Let's get out of here." Casey staggered to his feet, wobbled his way out of the cubicle, and collapsed. "Oh, Jeez, what have they done to you?" Scott whispered, his voice tattered.

Then Cristina was beside him, stroking Casey's head as she whispered, "You carry the rear end, I'll get the front." She scooted her left arm under Casey's chest and cradled his head in the crook of her right arm.

Following her lead, Scott started to wrap his arms around Casey's hindquarters. "No," whispered Cristina. "First wipe your fingerprints off the latch and doorknob." Scott just looked at her. "Do it!" she hissed.

113

Her command shifted Scott into gear. Pulling down the sleeve of his sweatshirt, he closed the cage door and rubbed at the cage latch and the cubicle's doorknob. Then, as quietly as possible, the two of them picked up Casey and headed out of the room. They had just made it into the hallway, wiped off the door handle, and had turned left, when a hand came down on Scott's shoulder and a hoarse voice snarled, "Gotcha!"

If he'd been an old man, Scott told himself later, he might have dropped dead from fright when that hand clamped onto his shoulder. Instead, he squeaked and nearly dropped Casey. At Casey's other end, Cristina let out a yelp, like a dog hit with a pellet gun, but she, too, held on to Casey.

Whoever had grabbed him had let go of his shoulder but was still behind Scott, so he couldn't see who it was. At first he thought it was the guard, because the voice was familiar. Then he dismissed that idea because he would have heard the guard's boots clumping down the hall.

Jackson! Scott thought next, his heart almost bursting out of his chest. Jackson must be working late. Scott turned as far as he could without letting go of Casey, and as he did, the figure said, "Decided to join us after all, eh? I never would have guessed." And even before he saw the face, Scott knew the voice.

"Mr. ... Mr. ... Peter!" he said. "What are you doing here?"

"Same thing as you, apparently. Freeing some of these poor, mistreated animals. I never would have figured you to have the guts to do it though."

"I'm not ... I mean ... I'm not freeing the animals," Scott sputtered. "I know this dog is all."

"What's going on out here?" Another figure came up behind Peter. Marcy. She held a cat in her arms.

"I found these kids giving us a hand," Peter whispered. "Why didn't you tell me he'd come around to our side? He the one who gave us the key?"

Gave them the key? wondered Scott. What key?

"Shut up, Peter," Marcy snapped. "This kid—Scott, isn't it?—doesn't know squat about any of this."

"He must know something. He did us a favor, didn't he? Delayed that guard long enough to give us time to warn everyone to keep quiet."

"Blind luck," said Marcy. "He didn't know we were in here."

"Well, then," said Peter, "what are we going to do about him—and his girlfriend there? They're witnesses. They could squeal on us."

Marcy came closer and stood beside Casey. "What *are* you doing here?" she asked.

Cristina spoke up first. "This is my great-aunt's dog," she said. "She gave him to the pound to be adopted, but when Scott found him here, we decided to rescue him."

Marcy stroked Casey's head. Scott saw she was wearing gloves. "The Carleton pound does sell animals to labs," she explained, "but never to a lab in the area." She scratched Casey gently behind his ear. "A broker must have gotten him," she said. "Sometimes they go around to different shelters pretending they want to adopt. Then they sell the animal to a lab. Lucky fellow," she said. "You're getting out—along with this little guy here." She patted the cat's head.

"You mean you'll let us take him?" Scott asked, blood pounding at his temples.

"We can't just let them walk out!" Peter said.

115

"What are they going to do?" Marcy asked. "Run to the police and say 'When we broke into I.B.L. tonight to steal this dog, there were some people from A.R.F. there too, letting animals out of cages.' Is that what they'll say? Sure, Peter."

"I just hope you don't blow it on this one, *Ms. Niven,*" snarled Peter. "This isn't exactly an area where you've had any experience. Marching around in circles chanting is more your thing." He reached out and grabbed Scott's shoulder again, giving it a painful squeeze. "When you come into work tomorrow afternoon," he said, "you better act real surprised when you hear about what happened tonight. If you know what's good for you."

Scott nodded. Then, without thinking, he said, his voice snotty, "I thought A.R.F. didn't do anything illegal or violent."

"Illegal, yes, violent, no," said Marcy. "But then, we think it should be illegal to torture animals, even for the benefit of humans. And saving animals from torture and letting a few hundred others scamper around for a night isn't violent." She moved ahead of them down the hall toward the back door. "You'd better leave now, before the guard comes back and catches you making a getaway. Good luck with that fellow. I hope he's okay. He doesn't look so good to me, even in this lousy light."

Cristina and Scott followed Marcy toward the exit.

"Remember to keep your mouths shut," Peter called after them in a hoarse whisper.

"Scott," Marcy said then, "we need to talk. About A.R.F." She nodded toward Cristina. "You, too." She held the door open until they were outside. "Come and see me—soon. You know where to find me."

"Probably in jail," Cristina whispered as the door clicked shut behind them.

Scott silently agreed with Cristina. He only hoped he and Cristina wouldn't be in there with Marcy.

The rain had let up a bit. I wish I'd thought to bring a blanket to wrap Casey in, or even had a jacket to put over him, Scott thought, as he and Cristina started across the lawn with their load. But I was expecting Casey to walk home on his own. Once he was free, I was expecting Casey to be—Casey.

But he wasn't. Not now. Perhaps not ever again. When Scott realized that, he wanted to bury his head in Casey's golden coat and howl. Instead, he plodded along behind Cristina toward the hawthorn bushes where Tim waited, glad it was dark and raining so that Cristina couldn't see the tears dribbling down his face.

Chapter Seventeen

"I thought you were never going to come out," Tim said when they reached him. "What happened? Why are you carrying him?"

"Later," answered Scott. "Let's just get him home and out of this rain." Already Casey's coat was plastered to his sides. "Here, you take this end," he told Tim. "I want to carry his head for a while." He touched Cristina on the shoulder. "You grab my bike when we get to it."

Taking turns pushing the bike and carrying the limp Casey, they headed toward Scott's house. Whenever it was his turn with the dog, Scott insisted on carrying Casey's front end. "Don't worry," he murmured, trying to keep the dog's head from drooping. "You're safe now. No one is going to hurt you again. Good dog. Good Casey." Finally they were at Scott's front door. At that moment the rain stopped.

"Great timing," muttered Tim, who looked as though he had crawled out of a storm sewer.

"Let's take him to my room," said Scott.

"I know we agreed to bring him here, but is this

such a good idea?" Tim asked. "Won't your dad be home in the morning?"

Scott shrugged. "I don't know when he'll be home. Besides, I can't worry about that. I'll keep Casey in my closet like we planned. It's a walk-in, so it's big enough," he explained to Cristina. "If my dad finds him, he finds him, but I think Casey should be where I can watch him."

The boys collected newspapers and old blankets for the closet floor while Cristina rubbed Casey with a towel. "Have you got a hair dryer?" she asked. "He's still damp."

When Casey was dry, Scott tried to get him to eat some leftover meat loaf, but all he wanted was water. He drank lying down, with Tim propping his head up and Scott holding the bowl to his mouth. When he'd had enough, he licked Scott's hand, sighed, and stretched out on the blanket.

"I can't figure out why he's so weak," said Cristina. "I checked him all over and couldn't find anything wrong. He didn't have an operation or anything."

"Maybe they gave him some medicine they're testing and it made him sick," Scott suggested, stroking Casey's head. He heard a choking noise and looked up to see Tim's face crumple.

"Dr. Wilder's my uncle," Tim said, his voice splintering. "I can't believe he'd do this to animals."

"I can't believe *anyone* would do this to animals," said Cristina. She poked Scott. "You know what that A.R.F. woman said about going to talk to her. I think I'll do it. A future reporter should learn about a zillion different things. And now that I've seen A.R.F. in

119

action inside a lab I could even write about that some day."

Her words caught Tim's ear, distracted him. "What do you mean, 'inside a lab'?"

"Oh, right, we forgot to tell you," Cristina said. "We weren't the only ones inside I.B.L. tonight. That's why we took so long. A.R.F. was in there. They caught us taking Casey."

"What?! They did? Oh, no, that's terrible."

"No, it isn't," said Cristina. "It's perfect."

"Perfect?!" Both Tim and Scott stared at her. Scott wondered if her brain had gotten soggy from too much rain.

"Of course." Cristina looked disgusted. "Don't you see? If only one dog—Casey—was missing, it might be easy to figure out who took him, especially if Marcy's wrong and the pound did sell Casey to the lab. But now, he'll be just one of a whole bunch of animals. No one will think much about it."

"But what is A.R.F. going to do about us?" Tim asked.

"Nothing, of course. It was a standoff. None of us was supposed to be there, so, for sure, none of us is going to rat on the others."

"But what were they doing?" Tim asked.

"Letting animals out of cages, I think," Scott told him. "And stealing some of them. Marcy had a cat."

Tim groaned. "I guess my parents will be getting a call first thing in the morning for my dad to come and see the mess so he can figure out the insurance." He sat up straighter. "Gee, maybe I should go along. Sort of as a spy. That way I can find out how much the lab knows and what the police are going to do."

"Great idea," Scott said. "That means you'll have to be home early though."

"Yipes!" Cristina was looking at her watch. "It's nearly one-thirty in the morning. Sometimes *Tia*"— she looked at Tim—"my great-aunt, gets up in the night. And she always checks on me when she does. I know, because she wakes me when she flushes the toilet. And usually it's around two. So I have to scram." She gave Casey a pat and jumped to her feet. "I'll come over in the morning to see if there's anything I can do," she finished. "For sure I'll stay with him while you're at work."

"Cristina," Scott called, as she started toward the bedroom door.

She stopped, looked back.

Scott swallowed, then said, "Thanks. For, you know, helping out. I was . . . glad I wasn't alone in there tonight."

Cristina nodded. "But I didn't do it for you. I did it for Casey." She shrugged. "And I did it because it'll help me be a great reporter someday. A great reporter can never have too many experiences." The words were spoken in Cristina's usual snappy tone. But she grinned at Scott over her shoulder as she went through the door.

"Thanks, anyway," Scott called, as he stood up, yawned. "Hey," he told Tim, "let's get into dry clothes and then you can crash. You look beat."

"You do, too," said Tim, as the boys started to change.

Scott shook his head. "I am, but I think I'll keep an eye on Casey for a while. First I'm going to go down and grab some food and make sure that crazy Cristina locked the door behind her."

121

A few minutes later Scott was back, his hands full of potato chip bags and soda bottles. "I almost forgot to give you those keys we took," he said, as he came through the bedroom door. "You'll have to sneak them back into the cookie tin tomorrow. With A.R.F. getting into the lab tonight, it would be a real mess if your parents found the I.B.L. key gone." He set the snacks down, walked over to where he'd dropped his wet jeans, and started to dig into the pocket. Then he stopped.

"Tim!" he said. "I just remembered something else. When we were in the lab tonight, Peter—one of the A.R.F. guys—said something to Marcy about how he thought *I* was the one who had given A.R.F. the key. He must have meant the key to get into the building. You know what that means?"

Without waiting for an answer, Scott went on. "It means A.R.F. has a spy inside the lab. Someone who works there gave them the key. I wonder who it could be?"

He waited for a reaction from Tim, but when his friend didn't answer, he peeked into the closet and re-alized no reaction would be coming. Tim was stretched out on the closet floor beside Casey, sound asleep.

Scott crammed the loose keys into Tim's soggy jeans pocket, then turned out the overhead light, leav-ing only one small desk lamp glowing. He shook his head and muttered, "You could have left me more room," as he scrunched down on the other side of Casey and started to munch chips. I'll get in bed after a while, he told himself. But a few minutes after he'd finished eating, he, too, was asleep beside Casey.

* * *

122

Scott woke early, shortly after sunrise. Quickly he checked Casey. Then he poked Tim. "Wake up," he ordered. "Listen."

"What? What?" mumbled Tim, rubbing at his eyes and patting around the floor for his glasses, as though without them he couldn't hear.

"Listen to him. He sounds . . . snuffly, doesn't he?"

Tim slid his glasses onto his face, then bent over and put his ear next to Casey's nose. Casey raised his head slightly and nuzzled Tim's ear. Tim listened, then nodded. "Yeah, he does. Like he has a chest cold or something. His nose is dry too," he added, touching Casey's nose.

"That doesn't always mean anything," Scott told him. "But I sure don't like the sound of that rattle when he breathes. What do you think we should do?"

"Take him to a vet?"

"Oh, sure. Take him to a vet. Real smart."

"Well, what do you expect, asking me questions before I'm even awake." Tim paused, then asked, "How about a vaporizer?"

"Yeah," said Scott. "That might help. That's what Mom uses when Julie and I get a cold."

As he mentioned Julie's name, Scott shivered. He'd hardly thought of her since they'd left the lab the night before. "They probably have the results of Julie's tests by now. I sure hope she's okay," he said, trying not to feel too guilty for forgetting her.

"Aw, she's probably fine—better than Casey," Tim said. "Hey," he added, "before I go home, don't you think I should help you carry Casey outside so he can . . . you know."

"Cripes, I hadn't thought of that," Scott said. "You're right. But let's see if he can walk first.

Maybe he's stronger today." He reached down to coax Casey to his feet and noticed he still had a collar around his neck with a metal tag hanging on it. The tag had a number on it. Scott undid the collar and tossed it into the back of his closet. "Come on, Casey," he said. "Wanna go outside?"

Casey's tail thumped the floor and he shifted position, as though trying to gather enough strength to rise. The boys whooped when Casey raised himself on his front legs, then his back legs and staggered after Scott, but it made Scott's heart ache to watch him. "Never mind," he said, knowing the dog would never make it down the stairs. He gestured to Tim to take Casey's hind end. "One free ride coming up."

Outside, a wispy morning fog clung to the rooftops. The grass, wet from last night's rain, sparkled with diamond drops. The boys set Casey down next to the jacaranda tree, wondering what to do next. But once again Casey rose on his front legs, and again managed to get his back legs under himself. He didn't have enough energy to raise his hind leg though, so just peed where he stood.

"He seems a bit stronger," Tim said when they were carrying Casey back upstairs. "I think he's getting better."

"Yeah," said Scott, but he wasn't so sure. Perhaps it had been a mistake taking Casey from the lab. No, he decided. If he's sick, it's better for him to be sick around people who care about him. And no matter what they were doing to him at the lab, for certain he would have ended up dead, sooner or later.

A few minutes later, Casey was nibbling at some of the meat loaf, and Scott knew rescuing him hadn't been a mistake. Casey was going to be fine. "Good boy," Scott praised him. "That'll get your strength up."

"I'll let you know what happens about the lab," Tim told Scott as he got ready to leave. "And don't forget to use the vaporizer."

"Don't forget to put those keys back as soon as you get home," Scott reminded him. Then he slapped himself on the forehead. "I almost blew it!" He pointed at Tim's pockets. "Empty them! Your pockets!"

Tim curled his lip, but did as he was ordered. As he held out the fistful of loose keys, Scott snatched at the one with the round, white paper tag dangling from it.

"The hall key I took from the lab," he explained. "I've got to put it back. I stuck it in your pocket last night with the keys from your pantry."

"Lucky you remembered," said Tim, heading down the stairs.

Then Tim was gone and Scott was alone with Casey. What if he doesn't get better? he wondered, as he went into the kitchen to get himself some breakfast. What'll I do then? He was still thinking about that when his father's car turned into the driveway.

Yikes! thought Scott. It's just past 7:30. I didn't think he'd get here for hours.

He raced up the stairs and closed his closet and bedroom doors, then raced back down, wondering if his father would ask him why he was home from Tim's already.

Scott was sitting at the kitchen table when Mr. Richmond came through the door. Scott noticed the dark circles under his father's eyes and the deep lines running from his nose to the corners of his mouth. He looked as though he hadn't had any sleep. And he looked upset.

It's bad news, Scott thought. Bad news about Julie. But before he could ask about his sister, his father gave him a hard look and asked, "Just what kind of a stunt do you think you're trying to pull? Did you really think you'd get away with it?"

Chapter Eighteen

Dad found out about us taking Casey, Scott thought. He felt his insides go all soft and squishy. If Dad knows, someone else knows too. Juvie Hall, here I come.

He heard a noise, realized he was cracking his knuckles, and sat on his hands. Wondering what to do, he remembered his encounter with the guard at I.B.L. the night before. If he could handle the guard, he could handle his dad—he hoped.

Scott looked his dad in the eye. "I'm sorry. I didn't think anyone would find out."

Mr. Richmond shook his head. "We wouldn't have found out, except that I went by the Wilders' to talk to you this morning. Instead, I had a good talk with Tim's mother. She had some interesting things to tell me. Seems you lied to her, in addition to all the other nonsense you pulled."

"But you were all busy with Julie . . ." Scott started to explain.

"You didn't even tell Tim's mom about Julie. All part of your scheme, I suppose. And that's what really ticks me off. Your mother and I have enough to worry about with Julie right now, without you pulling stunts like this." Mr. Richmond's voice had been getting louder and louder and now, with each word, he slapped the table next to Scott. "The—NEXT—time—you're—told—to—STAY—at—TIM'S—HOUSE, you—STAY—at—TIM'S—HOUSE."

Scott's entire body went limp. Dad doesn't know about Casey, he thought with relief. He's mad because Tim and I spent the night alone here—and told some lies to do it.

"I'm really, really sorry," Scott mumbled. "I . . . just wanted . . . to be close to home last night, but I didn't want to be alone, and I knew if we asked Tim's mom she wouldn't let us stay here, just the two of us. So we . . . lied. It won't happen again." He waited, silent, wondering what punishment his father would decide upon.

But all his father said was: "You're right, it won't happen again. You'll be spending nights at Tim's for a while and I'll be checking on you to make sure you're there."

Scott got a watery feeling in the pit of his stomach when he realized what his father had said. "What's going on?" he asked. "Aren't you and Mom coming home? Isn't Julie coming home? Isn't she okay?"

All the air seemed to go out of Scott's dad. He slumped in his chair and rubbed the back of his neck, then his forehead. "That's why I went to Tim's to talk to you," he said. He reached over and took Scott's hand. "There's good news and bad news. The bad news first."

Scott held his breath, hoping he wasn't going to hear what he thought he was going to hear.

128

"Julie has leukemia," his dad said, his voice ragged.

He was silent until Scott said, "You said there was good news too." Even to his own ears, Scott's voice sounded teary.

"The good news is that it's not the most serious kind. The doctors say she has a good chance to recover."

It was a moment before Scott trusted his voice enough to say, "I *know* she'll get better." Then in a quieter voice, "Won't she, Dad?"

Mr. Richmond let go of Scott's hand and drew himself up straighter in his chair. "Of course she will," he said. "But it's going to be tough for a while. Your mom will stay at the hospital with her as much as possible. I'll drive up every night after work to give your mom a break and keep her company. Your mom might come home some nights. Or maybe not. Maybe we'll rent a motel room or something." Mr. Richmond almost seemed to be thinking out loud. "There are other hospitals closer, but we want the best." He shook his head, as though trying to bring himself back to Scott. "Anyway, that's why you'll have to stay with Tim. If things go on too long, we'll ask Grandma and Grandpa to come, but I don't think that's necessary yet."

"So what happens now?"

"Julie starts treatment right away. Today."

"What kind of treatment?"

"They're going to give her real powerful drugs. Chemotherapy, it's called." Mr. Richmond ran his hand through his hair and rubbed his neck again.

"For how long?" Scott asked.

His dad shook his head. "I don't remember half of

129

what the doctor said last night. I think he said we'd know in about a month if the drugs are working. But I don't remember if he said she had to take them that long." He sighed. "It was just too much," he muttered. "Too much."

A whole month, Scott thought. The summer would be almost over by then. "Will she be able to start kindergarten in September?" Scott asked. Julie had been talking about kindergarten for as long as Scott could remember. She started most of her sentences with the words, "When I'm a big girl and go to kindergarten . . ." Scott knew if Julie didn't start kindergarten when she was supposed to, it would break her heart.

"We'll have to wait and see," Mr. Richmond said. "But I think she will. And to make it happen, I'm going to give you a job. Some people think that if a person has a dream or a wish, he should get a picture in his head of that dream coming true. And then it will. So your job is to picture Julie walking through the door to kindergarten class on the first day of school. In your picture she's smiling and she looks as healthy and bouncy as."—Scott's dad gestured with his hand, searching for a word—"as a . . . oh, as she looked before all this started." His voice sounded thick. "Can you handle that?"

Scott's throat felt swollen, so he didn't try to speak, just nodded. He closed his eyes and instantly saw Julie the way his father had described her. She was even wearing her favorite denim jumper and pink polo shirt.

Scott smiled to himself. This was going to be the easiest job his dad had ever given him.

Mr. Richmond pushed his chair away from the table and stood up. "I've got to shower and get back to the hospital," he explained. "I won't be going to work for a few days. Do me a favor, would you? Make me a couple of pieces of toast to take along. A banana'd be good too. Then find that cross-stitch thingie your mom's doing and put it in a bag with all that other stuff she uses when she's working on it. She needs something to do while she's sitting with Julie."

Scott nodded, then followed his father to the bottom of the stairs and watched until he had disappeared into the bedroom.

Don't bark, Casey, he thought, although he wasn't too worried about that happening. The dog didn't have enough energy to do much more than whimper. His dad wouldn't hear a whimper with the door closed and the shower running. Scott went to look for his mother's needlework.

When Mr. Richmond came downstairs a short time later with another suitcase of stuff for Scott's mother and Julie, his eyes were red, and Scott thought his dad had been crying again. Then he sneezed, blew his nose, and said, "Darn allergies. I'm all stuffed up. If I didn't know better, I'd swear there was a dog in this house. I've been sneezing ever since I got out of the shower."

The towel! Scott thought. After she had dried Casey, Cristina had asked him what she should do with the damp towel. He'd told her to hang it in the bathroom. But he hadn't said which bathroom. She must have put it in his parents'. And his dad must have dried himself with it. Holy burrito!

Mr. Richmond dabbed his eyes. "I peeked in your room and noticed some dirty clothes lying around, so maybe if you washed them, it would help. If I know

131

you, I'll bet you haven't been changing into your dog clothes every day."

When his father mentioned looking in Scott's room, Scott thought he was going to choke on the cereal he was chewing. "Sorry, Dad," he sputtered, once he'd gotten it down. "Sometimes I forget." Scott had some clothes he was supposed to wear only for walking the dogs. When he came home, if they didn't need washing, he put the clothes into a plastic bag in his room so they wouldn't bother his dad. Lately he'd been forgetting. But Scott knew the clothes were only part of the problem. If his dad learned about the clothes *and* the towel *and* the dog, he'd figure Scott was trying to do him in.

Scott looked at his dad. "Maybe you should picture yourself petting a dog and not sneezing," he suggested, only half teasing.

His dad raised an eyebrow. "Maybe I should. Gotta run now." He gave Scott a quick squeeze around the shoulders. "I want you to promise me you'll report to Tim's mom right after you walk the dogs this afternoon," he said. "I'm not going to tell your mother about last night. Already she's worried about abandoning you. I know this is tough, but we really need you to cooperate this next while. No more stunts, okay?"

"I promise I won't do anything else to upset you," Scott said, and meant it. He'd already committed every sin he had planned to commit, so he felt certain he could keep his promise. "Say hi to Mom. And give Julie a hug from me. When can I go and see her?"

"Probably over the weekend," his dad replied, as

he went out the door. The last sound Scott heard before the door closed was his father's sneeze. At that moment, the house felt emptier than it had ever felt before.

Chapter Nineteen

Scott plodded up the stairs to his room. His brain felt as though someone had opened a hole in his skull and filled it with cold lead. His head was suddenly too heavy to hold upright and his thoughts came in slow motion. It was the way he felt if someone tried to wake him up at the exact moment he sank deepest into sleep. Over and over the same slow thought crept through his mind. Over and over and over. Ju-lie-has-leu-ke-mi-a. Ju-lie-has-leu-ke-mi-a.

He opened the closet door and sank down beside Casey, not even noticing the dog's quiet tail thump. For a long time he simply sat there, his mind blank.

At last Scott's brain started working again.

"I'm sitting beside your bed," Scott told the dog, "and Mom's sitting beside Julie's. Of the four of us, I'd rather be me. I know I wouldn't want to be Julie."

Scott ran his hand softly over Casey. A shiver rippled the dog's coat. "Your breathing is noisier," Scott said. Casey shivered again.

It's like he has chills, Scott thought, reaching for an extra blanket and gently covering the dog.

Scott's eyes were burning, so he closed them. As

long as my eyes are shut, I might as well follow Dad's suggestion of picturing a wish coming true, he thought. He imagined his sister walking into the classroom on her first day of kindergarten. Then he tried to add Casey to the scene, tried to see him trotting along behind Julie, his coat glowing, his eyes sparkling, his pink tongue hanging out. But Casey wouldn't appear, no matter how hard Scott tried to picture him.

Scott opened his eyes and glanced at his watch. "Almost 9:30. At least I don't have to go to work for a few hours yet. I hope you're feeling better by that time."

He held the bowl of water near Casey's nose, then supported the dog's head as he tried to lap some. Casey's raspy breath reminded Scott he hadn't set up the vaporizer.

Good thing I didn't do it before. I would have had a terrific time explaining *that* to Dad, he told himself, just as Casey shuddered again.

Scott set down the water bowl. Again he closed his eyes and tried to imagine Casey acting like his old self, chasing after a ball and playing tug-of-war with his leash. Again Scott couldn't form a picture of a healthy Casey in his mind. Every time he tried, he saw Julie. I guess it's more important to think good thoughts about Julie, Scott decided. He tried to drag his eyes open so he could go get the vaporizer, but he felt as though some of that lead in his brain had oozed onto his eyelids and was holding them closed.

"Have to get the vaporizer," he mumbled, just as he fell asleep.

While he dozed, Scott dreamed about his visit to the lab the night before. But this time it wasn't Casey he was rescuing, it was Julie, and she wasn't in the cage where he thought she should be. After a frantic search through the lab, he found her lying on an operating table with Dr. Wilder about to give her an injection from a gigantic needle. She gazed at Scott with wide, accusing eyes, as though to say, If you'd been nicer to me, I wouldn't be here now.

Scott snapped awake just as he grabbed for Dr. Wilder's imaginary needle. He shook his head, trying to erase the terrible picture his dream had sent him.

It wasn't real, he told himself, and it's *not* my fault Julie's sick. As though to reassure himself he was awake, he reached under the blanket and rested his hand on Casey's side. "You're breathing's worse," he said to the dog. "And you're hot."

Quickly he pulled the blanket off Casey. Then he smacked himself on the forehead. "The vaporizer, you mush head." He pushed himself to his feet and hurried to the bathroom to find it.

He was rummaging around in the cupboard under the sink when a thought struck him that left him feeling as though a bully had slammed a fist into his gut, a thought that should have struck him much earlier: if he had to sleep at Tim's, Casey would be alone all night every night.

But he can't be! Scott thought, his brain once again in full gear and panic rising. I have to be with him. What if he needs to go outside, or needs a drink and can't lift his head? He can't be alone all night. He just can't be.

Easy, he told himself. Casey's only got chills and a fever. He probably caught cold from being wet last night and'll be better before you even go to work. Most fevers don't last long.

Hah! What do you know? another part of his mind answered. Look at Julie. All she had was a fever too.

That's dumb, he told the doubting voice in his mind. Casey doesn't have leukemia. So shut up!

The voice did, but that didn't ease Scott's worries. Casey still can't be left alone, he decided, sticking his head into the cupboard to grab the vaporizer. I'll just have to convince Mrs. Wilder it would be okay for me to stay home alone. But even as he decided that, he knew it was hopeless.

The doorbell rang and Scott jumped, hitting his head on the inside of the cupboard. For a second, he thought about not answering it, afraid it might be the police wanting to question him about the break-in at the lab. Even if they didn't suspect him, they might want to grill every person who worked there.

The bell rang again. His heart loose inside his chest, Scott stood up. Then he heard a faint voice call, "You dead in there—or what?" Cristina.

Scott pounded down the stairs.

"Finally," said Cristina, when he opened the door. "How's Casey?"

"Not so good," Scott told her, standing aside to let her in. "A while ago he was shivering, now he feels like he's burning up."

Cristina pointed to the vaporizer. "What's that for?"

"He's breathing kind of funny. Like he has a cold in his chest."

"Maybe he does. He got pretty wet last night."

"That's what I was thinking too." He led the way to the stairs. "You get home okay?"

"Yeah. *Tia* didn't get up until after I was in bed.

How about you? Any problems besides Casey not feeling good?"

"I got caught," Scott told her as he led her up the stairs. "My dad went to Tim's to see me this morning and found out I didn't spend the night there."

"Did your dad find Casey?"

"No." He was about to tell her his dad wasn't going to be coming home at night—and why, but he held back, not wanting to say those three terrible words out loud: Julie has leukemia. Thinking them to himself was one thing. Saying them out loud, another.

I'll tell her after I've set up this thing, he decided, filling the vaporizer, then leading Cristina toward the closet. But when he saw Casey, the vaporizer dropped from his hands and he stumbled over it as he covered the few steps to where the dog lay.

"What's wrong with you?" he yelled, kneeling beside Casey. "What's wrong with you?"

Chapter Twenty

Casey's eyes were open, but rolled back in his head. His teeth were bared, and his body was jerking, as though filled with a thousand springs coiling and uncoiling in random sequence. First his front legs shook, then his head jerked, then his back legs twitched. Then he was still, before his entire body shuddered and the jerking started again.

"What's wrong?" Scott yelled again, his eyes blurred, not noticing Cristina crouching beside him. He flung himself over Casey, hoping his weight would stop the jerking. Then suddenly it seemed as though he wasn't holding Casey. It seemed he was holding Julie.

"Julie," a voice pleaded. "Oh, Julie. Don't die. Please don't die. Somebody, help. Somebody, please help." It was his voice.

The jerking stopped and suddenly Casey became Casey again. For a moment Scott was afraid to move. If he got up, Casey might start shaking again. Or perhaps he was dead. He felt Cristina's hand on his shoulder, pulling him away.

"Convulsions," she said. "He was having a convulsion. It's over now."

Scott sat back and looked at Casey. He seemed to be sleeping. His side rose and fell slightly as he breathed, and a shiver rippled his coat, but otherwise he was still. Then Scott smelled a sour smell and noticed Casey had peed.

"A convulsion," Cristina said again. "My baby brother Mario gets one every time he has a high fever. It scares my mom half to death, but it doesn't seem to bother my brother. By the time my mom gets the doctor on the phone, it's all over and Mario is asleep."

Scott's eyes met Cristina's. She nodded. "It's probably just the fever. He'll be okay. It's lucky I can dog-sit while you're working, though. You wouldn't want to leave him alone. Come on, now. I'll help you clean up the mess. Where can I get dry newspapers?"

Scott took a deep breath and pushed himself up. By the time the closet was clean and the vaporizer was running, he felt calmer.

Scott sat on the edge of his bed. Cristina was on the floor, back propped against the wall outside the closet door, feet in her white high-top sneakers sticking straight out. "You know what you said earlier . . . about not leaving Casey alone," Scott began.

"Yeah." Cristina started twisting one of her ponytails around a finger.

"Well, there's a problem. If Casey stays here, he'll be alone all night, 'cuz I have to sleep at Tim's house."

Cristina whistled through her teeth. "Why? Aren't your mom and dad coming home?"

Scott shook his head. "They have to stay with Julie."

Cristina stopped twisting her hair, but she didn't unwind her finger. "Is she . . . ? Does she have . . . ?"

Scott nodded. He felt his face crumple and started rubbing his cheeks as though the motion could hold off tears.

Cristina took her hand out of her hair, put both hands in her lap, and stared at them. "I'm sorry. When you called the dog Julie, I sort of figured you'd had bad news about her."

Scott stopped rubbing his face. "Yeah," he said, looking down at the toe of his sneaker. He had hoped Cristina hadn't heard.

Cristina slapped her thighs, suddenly all business. "So, we have to find someone to come and stay with Casey. Either that or we'll have to find someplace else for him. Know anyone who can stay here?"

Scott shook his head slowly. It hurt to move. It hurt to think. "I guess we'll have to look for another place."

"Know what I think?" Cristina asked, her brown eyes narrowing.

"What?" Scott mumbled.

"I think we need some help. I think we need a grown-up."

"A grown-up!? Are you nuts!? And who do you suggest we get?" He jumped off his bed and started waving his arms in the air. "Maybe Dr. Wilder would be good. Yeah, Dr. Wilder would be good. Then he can have us thrown in Juvie Hall and he can go back to experimenting on Casey. Or wait! Maybe we should tell Tim's mom. Then *she* can tell Dr. Wilder. Or, better yet—my parents. They'd love to hear their son is a criminal. That's just what they need right now. Then they can go absolutely bonkers and I can spend the rest of my life visiting them in the loony bin." Scott stopped and stared at Cristina. "Are you nuts?" he asked again.

Cristina sighed. "I will be if I spend much more time around you. Just listen, will ya? I know exactly who *could* help, but she can't right now."

"Who?" Scott asked, interested in spite of himself.

"Marcy. She already knows about Casey and she probably even knows a vet who would take a look at him and not squeal to the police."

It was a good idea, Scott admitted. Why hadn't he thought of it? "So, why can't she? Help, that is?"

"Because she's at the police station answering questions about last night. She says there isn't any evidence to get her arrested, but the police will be watching her, so it wouldn't be a good idea for her to come here or anything. And, naturally, there's no way she can take Casey to her house."

"How do you know all this?"

Cristina leaned around the corner of the closet door to check on Casey. "I went over to the lab this morning. I talked to her for a while before the police asked her to go to the station." Her eyes got wide. "You should have seen the place. There were police cars all over. Tim got there with his dad, but Mr. Wilder made Tim stay outside when he saw all the cops. Tim told me his uncle is on his way back.

"But never mind about that. You'll hear about it when you go to work."

"I won't be going if we haven't decided what to do with Casey," Scott grumped.

"There's only one grown-up left we can count on to help us," Cristina said then.

"Who?" Scott asked, hoping she wasn't going to suggest Peter.

"Tia."

She might as well have suggested Peter, Scott decided. "Mrs. Sanchez!?" he exploded. "You *are* nuts. Don't you realize how she'd feel once she heard Casey didn't get adopted, but had ended up at the lab? She'd hate herself."

"Yeah, she'd be pretty upset," Cristina agreed. "But don't you see? She'd also feel guilty. She'd be glad to help us just to make it up to Casey for sending him to the pound. She'd let us keep him at her house. All we have to do is get him there."

"I don't know." Scott shook his head. "We'll have to tell her we have Casey sometime, but not until he's better. Then we can tell her the people who adopted him changed their minds. What if we tell her the truth and she gets so upset she has a heart attack or something?"

"She won't. She's pretty tough, my *tia.*"

Casey whimpered and Scott hurried over to offer him some water in case he was awake. "I guess there's nothing else to do," he said. "I only hope you're right. I only hope your aunt doesn't drop dead from the shock."

"She won't," Cristina assured him. "Trust me."

Chapter Twenty-one

Scott's stomach rumbled. He looked at his watch. "Noon!" he said to Cristina. "I have to be at work in an hour. I'd better get going if I'm going to talk to your aunt before I go to work."

"Who says *you're* going to talk to her?" Cristina jumped to her feet and stood staring at him with her hands on her hips. "She's my family. I'm the one who should tell her."

Scott scrinched his eyes at her. "No, I'll tell her. It's bad enough she'll learn that Casey went to the lab. How do you think she'll feel if she learns her sweet little Cristina helped me break in and steal him?"

Cristina lowered her brows at him. "I wouldn't tell her I had anything to do with it," she snarled.

Scott shook his head. "You'd slip. You'd want to brag, just a little bit, about what a hero you are, and you'd say something that would give you away."

Cristina's shoulders slumped. She sighed. "Okay, have it your way. Just go easy, okay? And if she hasn't eaten, remind her I left her lunch in the fridge."

Scott nodded. "Want a PBJ before I leave?"

"Sure. I'll wait here and you bring it up."

Scott hurried downstairs and started slapping peanut butter and jelly onto bread as fast as he could. Suddenly he was impatient to get away, to hurry the clock toward the time he could take Casey to Mrs. Sanchez's house. But first you have to talk to her, he reminded himself as the phone rang.

"Hey, Muttman," said Tim, when Scott answered. "What's happening?"

"Cristina's here," he said, cradling the phone on his shoulder and pressing the sandwiches together. "And I'm leaving to talk to Mrs. Sanchez. We have to find somewhere else for Casey to stay 'cuz I have to spend the next few nights at your house and I don't want him left alone."

"I know," Tim said. "Mom told me. About Julie too. I'm really sorry."

"Yeah," said Scott quickly, not wanting Tim to go on about it. For some reason, he felt okay until people told him how sorry they were. Then he felt like bawling. It was better not to mention Julie too often. "What's going on at the lab?" he asked.

"My uncle's getting back this afternoon. I guess it was a mess this morning. Some animals were missing, but most of the rats and mice and rabbits were just turned loose. I think they're all back in their cages now though."

"Do you think we're . . . you know . . . safe?" Scott asked.

Tim was silent for a second, then whispered. "I think so—unless someone finds Casey and connects him with the lab. "About eight animals were missing," he continued in a normal voice. "The police don't think there's much chance of finding them. I heard one cop say these animal rights groups have so many contacts, the stolen animals can disappear into someone's home anywhere in the state and never be found."

"Good," said Scott. He slapped the sandwiches onto plates. "Meet me at my house after I get off work. And bring your wagon, okay? The big one."

"What for?" Tim asked.

Scott cleared his throat as if to say, Stop and think, Stupid.

"Oh, yeah," Tim whispered. "To help move . . . the load."

It was going to be tight, Scott thought, as he hung up the phone and poured two glasses of milk. First talk to Mrs. Sanchez, then work, then home, then take Casey to Mrs. Sanchez's, then walk the dogs in time to get to Tim's for dinner. He should get to the store for dog food too. Casey didn't want to eat now, but when he started feeling better, he would.

When Scott got back upstairs, Casey was still asleep.

"He doesn't feel quite as hot," Cristina said as he handed her her PBJ.

"If Marcy's at I.B.L. when I get there, I'll ask her if she knows a vet we can call, just in case he's not better when I get home," Scott told her.

"Good idea," Cristina agreed. "There has to be at least one vet around here who's a member of A.R.F. In fact, you'd think every vet would be." She took a bite of her sandwich. "Super. You make a mean PBJ." She set down her sandwich and looked at her watch. "You better get going. It's twelve-thirty. Darn. I wanted to tell you what Marcy said this morning. It

146

was really interesting. She even gave me the name of a book to read."

"Tell me later. Just remember to cover Casey if he gets shivery and fan him if he gets hot. Tim's bringing his wagon over later. He should be here before I get back." Scott knelt and rubbed his hand over Casey's head. "See ya later, buddy. Hang in there."

"Remember, tell *Tia* gently," Cristina reminded him. "Don't just blurt it out."

"I won't," Scott snapped. "What do you think I am, a jerk?"

"Your words, not mine," Cristina replied, as he left the room.

"Scott!" said Mrs. Sanchez after he knocked at her door a few minutes later. "Where's Cristina? She said she was going to your house." She put her fingertips over her lips as though expecting bad news, knocking away a couple of bread crumbs that clung there.

"She is at my house. She's . . . doing me a favor." The crack of his knuckles sent Mrs. Sanchez's gaze toward his clenched hands. He shoved them into his pockets. "Can I come in? I really need to talk to you."

The old woman backed up to let him in. "Of course. Let's go to the kitchen. I'm just cleaning up from lunch. Cristina left me the most delicious tuna sandwich. Goodness, I don't know how I ever got along without her. And I don't know how I'm going to manage when she goes home." She led the way in a slow shuffle toward the kitchen.

"Sit," she told him, clearing her dishes from the table and getting out a teacup. "Would you like some tea?"

147

Scott shook his head, wishing she'd settle so he could just tell her and get it over with.

At last Mrs. Sanchez was seated, her dark eyes peering across the table at him. "Now," she said, "what do you have to tell me?"

Break it to her gently, Scott reminded himself. You don't know CPR. "It's about Casey," he began.

"You've been to the pound. You found him!" Mrs. Sanchez clapped her hands together and her eyebrows rose in delight.

Quickly Scott shook his head. Then he nodded. "Well, yes, I did find him. But not at the pound. I found him at . . ." He stopped. Face it, he told himself, there is no gentle way to tell her. Just say it and get it over with. "I found him at I.B.L.," he blurted out. "He was being used in some kind of experiment. Last night we—Tim and me," he added quickly, "we sneaked over there and we . . . we took him. I have him at my house now. But he's kinda sick and I have to sleep at Tim's house because my parents aren't home and Casey can't be left alone, so we're wondering if maybe he couldn't . . . if he couldn't . . . come here."

Mrs. Sanchez's eyes and mouth had gotten wider and wider as he spoke. Now she let out a soft squeak, closed both her mouth and her eyes, leaned her elbows on the table, and buried her face in her palms. Scott studied the purple river of veins on the back of her hands while he wondered what to say next.

Mrs. Sanchez spoke first. "Are you telling me," she said, her voice muffled, "are you telling me that I gave Casey to the pound to be adopted and he ended up in some research experiment?" Her hands dropped

148

to the table with a thud and began twisting around each other. "Is that what you're telling me?"

Scott summoned his courage and looked her in the face. Her eyes were shiny bright and full of tears. "Yes," he told her.

"And now you want to bring him here."

Scott nodded. "So he can have someone with him all the time."

"You say your parents aren't home?"

"Yes, ma'am," Scott replied. "That's why I have to stay at Tim's." He waited for Mrs. Sanchez to ask where his parents were, and was relieved when she didn't.

"Well, that explains why you took him to your house. Couldn't have done that with your dad there." She took a sip of tea from her cup. Scott noticed her hand was trembling.

Please, please don't have a heart attack, he pleaded silently.

"Cristina know about this?"

Scott nodded.

"She in on it?"

Scott shook his head. "She didn't have anything to do with stealing him," he said quickly, the lie making his ears burn.

"Don't lie to me, son." Mrs. Sanchez's voice was soft. "I know my great-niece. If she knew about it, there would be no way you could keep her from joining in on your escapade. Not *that* one, you couldn't." She seemed to sink lower in her chair and Scott looked around for the telephone in case he had to call 911.

Then Mrs. Sanchez drew herself up. "I'm glad,"

149

she said. "It was my fault Casey got into that lab. And if I couldn't help get him out, I'm glad Cristina was there to help in my place. Now tell me, what's wrong with the dog and what do you want me to do?"

Chapter Twenty-two

Scott pushed his bike into the rack outside I.B.L. The place looked almost normal, quieter than yesterday. Only a couple of A.R.F. protestors marched through rain puddles in front of the building. One was Marcy. She must have been right when she told Cristina the police didn't have enough evidence to arrest her.

Scott bent over to lock his bike. I'll talk to her right away, he told himself, and get the name of a vet.

Whoa, peanut breath, he thought then. How would it look if someone saw you talking to an A.R.F. member right after she was questioned about the lab break-in? Get a grip.

As he snapped the lock, Scott heard a hoarse whisper behind him. "How's the dog?"

He peeked over his shoulder. Marcy. She had laid down her sign and was squatting, pretending to tie her shoelace. Scott fiddled with his lock some more.

"Not so good," he whispered back. "Convulsions. Know a vet we can call?" Scott stood up and pretended to set his bike straighter in the rack.

Marcy stood too. "Morris Koopson. Koopson with

151

a *K*," she hissed, her lips barely moving. "Office on Grand Avenue. Mention my name."

"Thanks." Scott waggled his fingers behind his back at her as he passed. Koopson with a *K*, Morris. He'd phone right after work if Casey wasn't any better.

Like the outside, things inside the lab seemed close to normal. He'd expected to see a few rats and mice still running loose, despite what Tim had said, but they were all in their cages. Even Joe. His bandage was off and Scott took a good look at the shaved spot on his back. It looked kind of red, but Scott couldn't see any bumps or lumps.

"Lucky fellow," Scott said to him. "No tumors this time."

Jackson waved his arm toward a push broom. "Need you to sweep the floor before you start the feeding," he said. "I've been too busy to get to it."

Scott knew it wasn't Jackson's job—or Scott's job—to sweep the floor. Automatically he looked down. He saw tiny black mouse and rat droppings scattered around the floor like punctuation marks on a page.

"Guess this place was pretty wild this morning, eh?" Scott asked, "what with all the animals loose. Must have been fun, matching mice to cages."

Jackson's next words stopped Scott's breath. "What do you know about that? And don't tell me you read it in the paper this morning, because it wasn't in there. And Wilder managed to keep it pretty quiet, so it hasn't been on the radio or TV."

"Well, I—I—I," Scott stammered, suddenly remembering Peter's warning to play dumb about what had happened. Too late.

"You what? Were here last night helping A.R.F.?" Jackson's eyebrows were bunched into an angry knot.

Scott's thoughts flew around inside his head like captured wasps dashing themselves against the sides of a glass jar. He'd given himself away. One stupid comment and he'd blown it. Think fast, he told himself, or you'll be the next person dragged down to the police station for questioning. The crack of his knuckles snapped his brain into gear.

"My friend Tim," he said. "Dr. Wilder's his uncle. Tim's dad handles Dr. Wilder's insurance. So Tim's dad had to come down here this morning. Tim came—came too. He told me what had happened. *That's* how I know."

Scott knew from the look on Jackson's face that he believed him. Scott started to breathe again.

"Oh, yeah. I forgot that's how come you got the job. For a minute there I thought maybe you'd helped A.R.F. out a bit."

"If there's a chance I might have to clean up a mess, I'm sure not going to help make it," Scott said, as he went to get the push broom. He wondered if he dared pump Jackson for any more information. Aw, what the heck, he decided, then asked over his shoulder, "What about the rest of the lab? Tim only told me about the mice and rats."

"Pretty much the same. The rabbits were turned loose. Four cats and three monkeys were taken. And one dog that belonged to some woman. But at least they didn't torch the place or smash stuff like some of those other crazy animal rights groups." Jackson snorted as he went back to his office.

Scott started sweeping. I sure didn't need this extra work today, he thought. Next, I suppose Jackson will run out of Coke again and ask me to go to the store. Well, I'll just say no. If he goes himself, I can put the hall key back. Otherwise I'll just have to watch for a chance to sneak it back.

Scott worked quickly, keeping an eye on Jackson to see if he headed for the rest room or out the hall door. But after he'd fed and watered the last rodent, Scott still had the key in his pocket. So what if I don't put it back today? he asked himself. No one knows I have it. If it's missed, they'll just think the person who gave the master key to A.R.F. took the hall key too. I wonder who that was, anyway?"

He signed out and headed for his bike. Marcy was gone. A.R.F. was taking a break in the shade. Cristina was waiting beside the bike rack.

Scott shuddered. If Cristina was *here,* that could mean only one thing. Casey didn't need her. And there were only two reasons why that might be true. Either Casey was completely recovered, or . . . Scott forced himself to think it. Or Casey was dead.

Cristina must have understood the look on Scott's face. Before he could even ask, she said quickly, "Tim's with Casey. He came over early with his wagon. I came here to . . . to walk home with you."

"How is he?" Scott asked.

"Casey? He's . . . about the same." Then, hardly even pausing for breath, Cristina continued. "Was it a mess inside? Did anyone say anything to you? Did you figure out who gave A.R.F. the key? Maybe I'll ask Marcy. I want to talk to her some more. She told me some things this morning that really got me thinking."

Scott was barely listening.

"Know what Marcy said?" Cristina went on, as

Scott unlocked his bike. "She said it's not only animals in research labs that suffer. She said farms and rodeos and circuses and zoos are just as bad. Farm chickens are crammed into wire cages and stacked on top of each other. Calves are put in wooden crates too tiny for them to turn around in. Later they're killed to make veal." By this time Cristina was waving her arms around like she was an angry mother trying to get her rotten kids to listen.

"Rodeo animals," she continued. "Marcy said they're treated mean and get hurt during the shows. Circus animals are made to do things animals should never do—like bears riding bicycles. Zoos . . . What did she say about zoos? Oh yeah, even the best zoos don't let animals live and behave like they would in their own home. And hunting. You should have heard what she said about hunting—and slaughterhouses. And even about the way people treat their pets!"

Scott looked at her and shook his head. "She sure flipped your switch, didn't she?"

Cristina kicked at a piece of gravel lying on the pavement. "Yeah. She gave me a lot to think about. She said something really interesting about lab animals."

Scott decided he'd better act interested, even though he was really thinking about Casey. Cristina had been a lot of help in all this mess. Paying attention when she talked was the least he could do. "What did she say?" he asked, wobbling on his bike from trying to go slowly enough to keep pace with her.

"Marcy said scientists say they use animals for testing because animal's insides are so much *like* people's. Then they turn around and say it's okay to use

155

animals that way because the animals are so *different* from us they don't feel pain like we do. So are they like us, or aren't they?"

By now Cristina was practically jogging to keep up with him, so Scott swung off his bike and pushed it along beside her. "I don't know," he answered, wondering why Cristina was suddenly so much more yappy than usual. *Perhaps it's because she's found an interesting topic to investigate,* he told himself. *But I'd sure like to get a word in so I can find out more about Casey,* he thought, before adding, "I'll have to think about it." He thought he'd be able to mention Casey then, but Cristina's mouth kept going.

"You never did tell me if anyone said anything to you or if you found out who the spy was," Cristina said. "The one who gave A.R.F. the key."

Scott shook his head. "I didn't even get the key *I* took put back. Jackson, the guy who works in the rodent room, jumped on me when I let slip that I knew what had happened last night, because it wasn't in the news yet. Lucky I had Tim for an excuse. Then Jackson told me about the animals that were taken. A few cats and monkeys. And he knew about Casey, because he told me one dog had been taken too. One dog that—"

Scott almost dropped his bike. "Holy tamale! I know who the spy is. I know it, but I don't believe it. Boy, he must be some actor. He sure had me fooled."

Cristina tugged on his arm. "Who? Who?"

Scott shook his head. "Jackson," he said. "It has to be Jackson."

"The guy who works in the rodent room with you?"

"Yeah, it's got to be. He said something that gave

him away. I didn't even think about it until just now. When he told me about Casey, he described him as a dog that belonged to some woman."

Cristina wrinkled her nose. "I don't get it."

"Think. How did Jackson know Casey belonged to a woman?"

"Because . . . because . . ." Cristina clapped her hands to her head. "Of course! Because last night, when they caught us, I told Marcy and Peter Casey was *Tia's* dog."

"Ri-i-ight. And there's no way Jackson could know unless Marcy or Peter told *him*. And there's no way they'd tell him unless—"

"Unless he was on their side," Cristina finished for him. "Hey," she added, "maybe you'd make a good investigative reporter after all."

"Whoopee," Scott muttered. "Now will you please tell me about Casey? You said he was about the same. What does that mean? He still having convulsions or what?"

It was as if Cristina's mouth had been a water faucet out of which ran a steady stream of words. And suddenly the faucet was cranked off. She was quiet. Too quiet. The silence felt like a heavy cloak settling around Scott's shoulders.

Scott wheeled his bike in front of Cristina, blocking her path and almost clipping her shins with the pedal. "So?" he demanded, peering into Cristina's face. For the first time since he'd met her, Cristina didn't match him look for look.

Then she spoke. "If you've got the name of a vet, I think you'd better call him. Casey started vomiting and having diarrhea."

"Why didn't you tell me?" Scott's voice rose to a shout. "Why did you say he was about the same?"

"I came here to tell you. But I couldn't make myself do it right away. I knew how upset you'd be. So I—I just yapped. Sometimes I yap when I'm nervous about doing something."

"You didn't yap last night," Scott accused. "Or weren't you nervous when Peter caught us in the hallway?"

"I said I do it when I'm nervous, not when I'm terrified," Cristina snapped. "You crack your knuckles. I yap. Get off my case." She dodged around Scott's bike, giving the tire a kick on her way past.

Scott's shoulders slumped. Vomiting and diarrhea. He felt a huge hollow spot open up in his gut. The vet. He had to get that vet!

He jumped onto his bike and caught up with Cristina. "Come back to my house, okay?" he said.

Cristina didn't flicker an eyelash at him.

"Look, I'm sorry I was rotten," Scott continued. "I'm just worried about Casey."

Scott thought he heard Cristina snort. "We're all worried about Casey," she said.

"I said I'm sorry."

"Fine. You're sorry. I'm sorry. We're all sorry."

Scott didn't know what else to say after that, so just told her, "I'm going ahead so I can call the vet. I'll see you at the house. Okay?"

Cristina's look softened. "Yeah, see you at the house," she said quietly, breaking into a jog again.

158

Chapter Twenty-three

The stench snapped at Scott's nose before he reached the top of the stairs. Tim met him at the bedroom door, shaking his head.

"Sorry about the mess," he said. "I guess we should have taken him outside and just stayed there with him. We did put plastic garbage bags under the paper though."

"Forget the mess," Scott said, hurrying to the closet, though the smell made him want to choke. At least Casey was lying on clean newspaper. Tim and Cristina had done a good job.

Casey whimpered when Scott knelt beside him.

"He looks smaller," Scott whispered, stroking the dog's head. "Like he's shriveling up." Leaning down, he curled his arms over the dog and placed his face against Casey's, feeling the soft fur under his cheek. He watched Casey's side rise and fall with each panting breath the dog took.

"Did ya get the name of a vet?" Tim asked.

Scott gave the dog a gentle stroke and kissed him behind the ear. "Yeah, I've got to call him right away," he said, rising. As he ran down the hall to his

159

parents' bedroom, he remembered Marcy telling him to use her name. He tried to recall her last name, but couldn't. He'd just have to hope the doctor knew who he was talking about.

"My name is Scott Richmond. Marcy told me to call Dr. Koopson about my sick dog," Scott said when the receptionist answered the phone. He must have used the magic words because the doctor came on right away.

"Is this the dog Marcy Niven told me about?" he asked.

"Yes," said Scott. "Can you come?"

"My partner is off sick today, so I won't be able to get out of here for at least another hour and a half, two hours. Is there any way you can bring him here?"

Scott slumped onto his parents' bed. "I don't think so," he muttered into the phone, his free hand crumpling a lump of bedspread. Suddenly he realized how much he missed his mom and dad. Why do they have to be gone now? he wondered. I could have told them. They would have understood. They would have helped.

Tim appeared in the doorway, his eyebrows raised in a question.

"You still there?" The vet's voice brought Scott up straighter. He took a deep breath, trying to get rid of the sting at the back of his eyes.

"Yeah, I'm just . . . thinking. I—I'll call you right back," he said, and hung up the phone.

Tim's eyebrows were still raised, his forehead rippled like corrugated cardboard. "Well?" His voice squeaked like it always did when he was worried.

The fingers of Scott's right hand slid over and clenched his left index finger. Crack! The sound let out some of his worry. He moved on to the next finger and gave it a satisfying pop. For once, Tim didn't bawl him out.

"The vet can't come for maybe two hours," Scott told Tim. "We have to take him there."

"We could call a cab," Tim suggested.

"Got any cash on you?"

Tim's black hair jiggled as he shook his head.

"Me neither," Scott said. "Besides, it'd probably be an hour before a cab even showed up. And what if the driver didn't take dogs, or asked too many questions?"

"You're right," Tim agreed. "We don't dare let an outsider know about Casey. You and Cristina could end up in jail."

"That leaves Mrs. Sanchez, who doesn't even own a car," said Scott.

"What about that A.R.F. woman you met?" Tim asked.

"Marcy?" For a brief moment Scott actually thought Marcy might be able to help. Then he shook his head. "She's probably at I.B.L., marching and waving her sign. No fast way to reach her. And she can't let herself be found with Casey, anyway. She'd go to jail for sure."

Just then they heard Casey gag. "Here we go again," Tim said, as he turned and raced down the hall, Scott right behind.

"Oh jeez. What did they do to him?" Scott groaned, kneeling beside Casey. He grabbed a nearby roll of paper towel and held some under Casey's mouth as the dog continued to vomit.

When he stopped, Scott and Tim looked at each other. "We've got to get him to that vet," Scott said.

161

Then, the same thought struck them at once and they said in unison, "The wagon!"

"Downstairs, in the laundry room," Scott said quickly, "there are some old rugs. Put them in the wagon. In the garage—boxes. Find one about the size of the wagon. If Cristina shows, send her up here. I'm going to phone the vet.

"I'll bring him there," Scott said when Dr. Koopson answered the phone. "Be there as fast as I can." He slammed down the receiver in the middle of the doctor's good-bye.

Would they get there in time? Scott wondered, as he raced back to Casey. The doctor's office was about five blocks past I.B.L. Nearly a mile away. Would Casey survive being hauled around? Tim's wagon was a big one, but would Casey even fit in it?

Don't think, Scott told himself. Act. First he wiped Casey off as best he could. Then he dipped his fingers in the water dish and dribbled as much as possible into Casey's mouth. He was wiping the dog's mouth again when Cristina bounded through the door.

"What do you want me to do?" she asked.

"Help me carry him downstairs," Scott said, shoving the roll of paper towel inside his shirt. Casey whimpered as Scott and Cristina boosted him into their arms. "Sorry," Scott whispered. "We'll try to be gentle. Just try not to barf or poop for a while, eh?"

"You going to leave the mess?" Cristina asked. "What if your dad comes home?"

"No time to clean it up," said Scott.

Outside, Tim was laying some rugs in the wagon. Four cardboard boxes, all different heights but the same size around, were sitting beside the wagon. "I wasn't sure what you had in mind for the box, so I brought all the ones I thought might work," Tim explained.

Scott and Cristina lowered Casey toward the wagon.

"He's too big," Scott said immediately. "He won't be able to stretch out on his side. He'll have to lie the other way."

Tim wrinkled his nose, shoved at his glasses. "What other way?" he asked.

"You know, like dogs usually lie. On their stomach, or whatever, with their head on their paws. They don't take up as much room that way."

"But how do we get him to lie like that?" asked Cristina.

"Good question," muttered Scott. Then he added, "Tim, you hold him around the middle so that his legs hang down. Then, Cristina and I will fold his legs as you lower him. Back end first, so he'll get the idea."

With some juggling and cursing from the humans and some whimpering from the dog, it got done. "Don't worry, you won't be like that for long," Scott whispered to Casey. "I'm just sorry you have to go to the doctor smelling like that. You were always the cleanest dog in the neighborhood. Now, I have to hide you."

Scott grabbed a box about two feet high. "This one," he said. "The flaps have already been cut off."

"That's why you wanted the boxes," said Tim, catching on. "I wondered. But why not just cover him with a blanket?"

"I don't want anyone to stop us and ask what's wrong or anything like that," Scott explained. "No one will ever look twice at some kids hauling a box on a wagon." He lowered the box over Casey, open end down. It was exactly the right width to fit snugly along the sides of the wagon, but a couple of inches too long. "Oh, no," Scott groaned.

"It's okay," said Cristina. "As long as it's tucked in at the back, it'll stay. I can hold it. And this way he'll get some air."

"Okay, then, let's go," Scott said.

They went as fast as they could, Scott pulling, Tim on one side, Cristina behind. At first they slowed for intersections, easing the wagon gently up and down curbs and around bumps and holes. Then they found it was faster and easier to simply lift the wagon over these places, so Tim moved back beside Cristina. At each curb or bump, Scott would haul up on the handle till the front wheels were off the ground. Tim and Cristina would lift the back.

Sweat dribbled down Scott's temples and from under his arms. He wondered how hot Casey must be under the box. Right then Casey started vomiting again and Scott called a halt.

Scott peeked under the end of the box, stuck his hand in and rested it on Casey's head until the dog stopped. Then he pulled the paper towel out from under his shirt and wiped the dog's mess. It was hard with the box raised only a few inches, but he did the best he could. When he finished, Casey licked weakly at Scott's hand. "Let's get going before someone wonders what we have in here," Scott said, laying the paper towel roll beside Casey and lowering the box again.

"He seems to have quit vomiting," Tim panted from his end of the wagon after they'd gone another three blocks. "For the moment at least."

As they raced with the wagon into and out of shade

164

and sunshine, through the spray of poorly-aimed lawn sprinklers, past kids chasing balls, kids riding skateboards, Scott couldn't help thinking how much Casey would have enjoyed this run a week ago. "You would have stolen that ball," Scott told the dog one time. He didn't know if Casey could hear him, but he wanted to let the dog know he was near, wanted him, in his sickness, to know he wasn't alone. Later, he said, "You would have watered that hydrant." Later still: "You would have attacked that sprinkler."

"*I'd* like to attack that sprinkler," Cristina wheezed as they neared the lane to I.B.L.

As they passed it, Tim gasped, "That's Uncle Jack's car just going down the lane. Glad we didn't get here thirty seconds sooner."

Moments later, they were nearing Grand Avenue. "Right, at the next corner," Scott said. Soon they were standing outside the North Coast Animal Clinic.

Cristina glanced at her watch. "Twenty minutes since we left your yard," she panted. "We make a good team."

Tim pushed open the clinic door and Scott pulled the wagon through, not even stopping to remove the box. You never could tell who might be in the waiting room. Maybe a cop questioning the vet.

Dr. Koopson was behind the counter, handing a form to the receptionist. When Scott gave his name, the doctor looked over at an old man, who was sitting in the waiting room holding a cat that was nearly as bald as his owner. "I've got an emergency here, Mr. Laporte," he explained. "I hope you don't mind if I take it first."

Mr. Laporte waved a gnarled hand. "No problem,"

165

he said making a slurping sound, as though trying to suck his teeth back into his mouth.

Dr. Koopson pointed down the hallway. "First door on the right," he said. "Wagon, too. That was a good idea, by the way."

Scott maneuvered the wagon into the empty examining room. Tim and Cristina squeezed in behind him. As Dr. Koopson lifted the box off the wagon and knelt to examine Casey, a thought struck Scott. He felt a knot tighten between his shoulder blades.

"I just realized we don't have any—"

"Money?" the vet finished for Scott. "No problem. I treat rescued animals for free. It's my contribution to the movement."

Behind Dr. Koopson, Tim gave a thumbs-up signal. "Thanks," said Scott. He grinned at Tim and Cristina. The knot between his shoulders loosened. Things were definitely beginning to look rosier. They'd gotten Casey to a doctor in time and it wasn't even going to cost any money.

"Now then, fella," the doctor said, "let's see what we can do for you. You're one lucky dog, you know, having friends like these." He looked up at Scott. "Marcy told me how you rescued him," he explained.

Scott nodded as Dr. Koopson put his hand under Casey's jaw, ignoring the vomit Scott hadn't been able to wipe off, lifted Casey's head, and with his other hand, raised one of the dog's eyelids. Casey didn't move or try to pull away.

"He's a good dog," Scott said proudly. "He never minds going to the vet. He never even jumps when he gets a needle."

"Yes, I'm sure he is a good dog," the doctor

agreed. He patted Casey and gently laid the dog's head down on his paws.

"So?" Scott's voice made it a question.

"The doctor needs to know his symptoms," Cristina said in a knowing tone, "before he knows how to fix him."

Dr. Koopson stood up, turned to the sink beside him, and ran water over his hands. "There's no need to tell me his symptoms," he said, his voice barely heard over the running water.

"Why not?" Cristina asked.

The doctor pumped some soap into his hands and started to scrub. He took a deep breath, then said, "Because there's nothing I can do."

"What do you mean?" Scott asked, anger shading his voice. All he and Casey—and Cristina and Tim too—all they had gone through and the vet wasn't even going to *try* to make Casey better?

Dr. Koopson dried his hands, turned, and leaned against the sink, his shoulders hunched, his hands shoved into the pockets of his white coat. He looked at each one of them in turn. Then he shook his head slowly and said, his voice cracking, "I am *so* sorry, but there's nothing I can do because—he's already dead."

Scott felt as though a boulder had plowed into his stomach. "But—but—" he sputtered, scarcely able to breathe. "Only a few minutes ago he was . . ." He looked away from the doctor to Casey. This time Scott looked, really looked at the dog.

Casey seemed to be asleep. Except his sides no longer rose and fell. Except he reminded Scott of a gigantic, hollow beetle shell he had seen once. Like

167

that shell, Casey looked completely emptied of life. What the doctor said was true. Casey was dead.

The silence that followed was louder than anything Scott had ever heard. He felt dizzy and grabbed the doorknob to steady himself, expecting to plunge to the floor in a burst of tears. Instead, he did nothing, felt nothing, as though, like Casey and the beetle shell, he were emptied of any ability to feel.

Then Cristina broke the quiet with a gasp and Tim with a gulp.

"I *am* sorry," Dr. Koopson said again, his eyes gentle. "I know how hard it is to lose an animal you love." Then he added, "Do you want me to take care of him for you?"

"Take care of him how?" It was Cristina. Her eyes looked glittery, but other than that she seemed okay. Yeah, Scott thought, Cristina will make a good reporter. Even when things are rotten she still wants the whole story. Then he wondered how he could be thinking about things like that with Casey lying dead in the wagon. Wondered how he could think at all with his brain numb with misery.

"I could arrange to have him cremated," Dr. Koopson was explaining. "You could come back and get the ashes for burial."

Cremate Casey? Scott thought, his brain beginning to work again. Burn Casey? He shook his head at the same time as Cristina.

"Will your parents help?" the doctor continued.

"My parents don't know we have him," Scott explained.

"My great-aunt knows," Cristina said, kneeling and stroking Casey's side. "She'll let us bury him in her yard. I know she will." She looked up at the doctor.

"Casey was her dog," she explained. "She gave him to the pound, thinking he'd get adopted."

Dr. Koopson sighed. "Gotta get a law passed. Pound seizure shouldn't be allowed."

Stiffly Scott knelt beside Cristina and smoothed Casey's ear. He looked up at the vet. "If we tell you his symptoms, will you be able to tell why he died, what was done to make him sick?" he asked.

"I can try. But do you really want to know?"

Behind the doctor, Tim shook his head no. Cristina and Scott nodded.

Ignoring Tim's head shake, Scott described Casey's symptoms: the weakness, the chills, fever, convulsions, diarrhea, vomiting. "I can't say for certain," Dr. Koopson said when Scott finished, "not without knowing what kind of research they're doing at I.B.L. Was he in an area marked Sterile?"

Scott remembered the signs outside the dog room and on the door of Casey's cubicle. He nodded.

"If that's the case, he might have had low immunity. A sterile area has to be kept free of germs because any germ could have made him sick. Maybe he caught pneumonia."

"But why would he have low immunity?" Scott asked.

"He might have received an overexposure to radiation."

"Radiation?" Cristina yelped. "You mean like from a nuclear bomb?"

The vet nodded. "Or from X-rays or radiation machines. Sometimes research animals are given total body irradiation to kill all their bone marrow."

Scott's throat closed up at the doctor's words, but he managed to ask, "Why?"

"Without bone marrow, there's no immunity—no defenses against germs. It's done because then the researcher can *give* an animal a particular disease he wants to study. Like cancer maybe."

"If we'd come sooner, would you have been able to save him?" Cristina again.

Dr. Koopson shook his head. "Not if he'd had total body irradiation. I might have been able to help him live longer, but the radiation sickness would have killed him eventually. If the researcher had been able to continue the experiment, however, he *might* have survived, depending on what was being tested. But the best thing *I* could have done would be to put him out of his misery. It's over now, regardless." He bent down and stroked Casey's head. "I bet he's chasing a rabbit in dog heaven right now," he said. He stood up, then opened a cupboard behind him and pulled out a blanket.

"Here," he said. "Forget the box." The doctor helped Scott gently tuck the blanket around Casey, then handed each of them some Kleenex, before giving the dog a final pat. "There," he said then. "I doubt anyone will notice what you're pulling."

Scott thought about what might happen if anyone did see Casey and asked what had happened. I'll tell them, he decided, even if I go to jail. Then, Scott, Cristina, and Tim thanked the doctor and left the clinic, taking Casey home.

Chapter Twenty-four

As Scott, Cristina, and Tim headed for Mrs. Sanchez's house, they automatically lifted the wagon at the curbs and bumps. "This is silly," Tim said at one intersection. "Bumps don't matter anymore."

"Lift the wagon," Scott snapped, and they lifted.

Scott felt himself begin to thaw as they walked. A huge bubble of sadness inside him was threatening to spew out of his eyes as tears and out of his mouth as howls of anguish. He closed his mouth tightly, vowing that Cristina would not see him cry again.

As they again neared the lane that led to I.B.L., Cristina spoke. "I just realized what Dr. Koopson said—when he was talking about whether or not he could have saved Casey. He said if the experiment had continued, there was a chance Casey would have been okay."

Cristina's words slammed into Scott's brain like a wrecking ball into a chicken coop. Until she spoke, he'd been able to ignore Dr. Koopson's words, pretending he'd heard wrong. But now that the words were out there, hanging in the air between them, they became real. It meant Dr. Koopson had really said them. It meant something too horrible for Scott to even think about. Dropping the wagon handle, he whirled on Cristina.

"You're saying we killed him!" he hissed, the hiss more menacing than a shout would have been. "You're saying we should have just left him there to get experimented on, no matter how rotten it was for him, 'cuz then they might have tested something on him that would have made him better. Well, I'm glad we didn't leave him there." He looked down at the covered dog. "We didn't kill him, we saved him. He may be dead, but at least he's not suffering anymore." He stopped, gulped for air. "We didn't kill him," he said, his voice dropping to a near whisper. He jerked his head in the direction of where I.B.L. squatted, a half block away. "Casey was as good as dead as soon as he arrived there. We didn't kill him, Wilder did."

Scott paid no attention to Tim's quiet gasp. He reached down and picked up the wagon handle. He felt as though his numb brain had been set on fire, as though all the sadness and anger he felt over Casey's death were in there bubbling and boiling like a witch's brew. "I think I'll show Wilder exactly what his researchers have accomplished with their wonderful experiments," he said, turning in at the lane leading to I.B.L. "I bet it'll make him real proud."

He had gone only a step down the lane before Cristina dashed up beside him. "You're crazy!" she said. "We'll both end up in jail."

"They don't really send kids to jail," Scott snapped, not slowing his pace.

172

"They send them to Juvie Hall," Cristina said. "Same thing. And I don't want to go there." She tried to grab the handle away from Scott, but he hung on.

"I won't mention your name," he said, stopping to pry her fingers off the handle.

"You'll slip."

Scott gritted his teeth, spoke through them. "Then you can write a book about it and get famous. It'd be a great start to your career."

Cristina let go of the handle. "So go ahead and be an idiot," she shouted. "But if you so much as flash my name across that stupid brain of yours, I'll—I'll . . . Her voice trailed off and she turned and headed toward the street.

Scott didn't look over his shoulder. He just started down the long lane again, the wagon bouncing along behind.

He almost didn't hear the words, they were spoken so quietly. "Please, don't."

Scott stopped and looked back. Tim was standing behind him. His face had that crumpled look of a person trying not to cry. Scott had seen Tim cry lots of times. They'd been friends forever. And every time it amazed him. First Tim's eyes would start to fill with huge, glistening tear globs. Magnified by his glasses, the globs would get bigger and bigger, until Scott thought they couldn't possibly stay in Tim's eyes any longer. Then suddenly one humongous tear would slip over the edge of each lid and down Tim's cheeks. Another huge tear would follow the first, not running together and forming a stream, but each tear separate, as though determined to hang on to its identity as long as possible.

173

And as Scott stood there looking back, clutching the handle of Tim's wagon, the wagon carrying Casey, two tears did just that. They oozed over Tim's eyelids and slid slowly down Tim's cheeks. Three breaths later, each tear was followed by another. "Please, don't," Tim said again, his voice sounding as though he had a bad head cold.

For one brief moment, Scott was tempted to ignore Tim, to turn and march on down the lane and through the parking lot, to barge into Wilder's office, fling the blanket off Casey, and call Wilder a murderer. Then Tim said again, "Please, don't. He's my family."

Family. One small word, but the sound of it drained all the anger out of Scott, leaving him limp and, oh, so very tired. Family. Scott knew how important a word it was. He'd learned that these past few days when he'd had to do without his. He wondered how his parents were. He thought guiltily of Julie.

Family. Tim's my family, too, Scott thought. And so is Casey. Casey isn't my dog, but he's been family as much as any human. Kneeling, Scott pulled the blanket away from Casey's head. The dog's eyes were closed, but his lips were pulled back enough to show a bit of his teeth. He almost looks as though he's smiling, Scott thought, the sight forcing a lump of sadness into the back of his throat.

He stroked Casey's ear. Then he looked at Tim. Tim's face didn't look as crumpled, but his eyes had that same pleading look the golden retriever's had had when Scott saw it in the lab cage.

Scott knew what he had to do. He nodded and

managed to say "Okay," before the lump in his throat exploded. Then he buried his face in Casey's neck and his tears flooded down and soaked the honey-gold coat of the dog he had loved.

Epilogue

734 Cactus Street
Carleton, California
September 16

Hi, Cristina!
I got your address from your great-aunt. I've got a lot to tell you. Stuff I've been thinking about and stuff I've learned. Mostly stuff about Casey.

I dreamed about him last night. He was playing ball with me, just like he used to. And he didn't want to quit, just like he used to. When I finally gave up and crashed, he even came and jumped all over me. It seemed so real it was spooky.

(I'll have to finish this later. Your great-aunt just called and wants me to go over and help her with something. She didn't say what.)

Later . . .
Back again. The reason your great-aunt called was because she wanted me to help plant an azalea by Casey's grave.

176

That was some funeral we gave him, eh? I really liked that poem you read. I can't believe you wrote it yourself. And *Tia* (she asked me to call her that) playing that song on the guitar. Boy, was I surprised! I didn't even know she could play. I'm just sorry you finished digging the hole before Tim and I got there. I should have helped.

Remember how awful it was when *Tia* made me tell my parents what we'd done, even though they weren't *too* ticked off? I guess because they had Julie to distract them. Well, that wasn't the worst of it. After you went back home (I guess by then they'd had time to think about it) they made me go and confess to Dr. Wilder. Talk about shaking-in-my-sneakers day! But, know what? It wasn't half bad. Wilder seemed more sad than angry. He even told me he never buys animals from our pound to use in research and that he'd gotten Casey from a broker, like Marcy thought. And the broker promised him that Casey had come from a different county. Anyway, he didn't even fire me, although I was kind of glad when school started and I got to quit.

Since then, I've been doing a lot of thinking about what happened this summer. All it's done is mix me up. Especially since I learned what research Casey was being used for. Jackson (yeah, that guy I worked with at the lab) filled me in. It's a long story, but since I don't feel like doing a bunch of stupid geometry homework, I might as well tell you.

I marched in a demonstration at the pound last week to protest pound seizure. (*Tia* did too, but I'll let her tell you about that.) Guess who else was there. Jackson! Dr. Wilder learned Jackson had given A.R.F. the key to the lab and he'd been fired, so he didn't have to hide how he really feels anymore. He told me that the lab was doing research on something called GVHD. That's graft-versus-host disease. (The only reason I know is because I wrote everything down.) I don't know much about it, but Jackson told me it's a disease that happens when doctors try to cure sick people by giving them a healthy person's bone marrow. The healthy marrow thinks the sick person's body is an enemy and tries to kill it—or something like that. Then the sick person gets sicker instead of better. I.B.L. is testing a drug that might prevent GVHD.

Anyway, Jackson told me Casey had radiation to kill off his own bone marrow. That's when we took him. If we hadn't, he would have gotten some new marrow. Then they were going to give him the drug to see if it would keep him from getting GVHD. So Dr. Koopson and you were right. Dr. Koopson was right when he said Casey might have lived if we hadn't tried to save him. You were right that we killed him. We did. He might have lived if he'd gotten the drug. I feel real awful about that.

I'm going to make up for it though. I have to, because of something else Jackson told me. He said that the people who the drug might help are people who need marrow transplants because they have leukemia. Yeah, leukemia. Like my sister Julie has. I bet your reporter's mind can guess how that news made me feel. Here I go and save Casey, but at the same time wreck an experiment that might save my sister's life. Cripes!

So now I'm going to make it up to Julie and to Casey. Julie's home now. She even started kindergarten this week. A bit late, but she didn't care. She looks kind of strange because her hair fell out from the treatments she's had. And she has to take all kinds of pills and junk and go for tests all the time. But at least we know the treatments worked, because Julie's in remission. That means her leukemia is gone for now. But it might come back. And here's where I come in. We're all going to have our bone marrow tested to see if it's like Julie's. If it is, she might get a transplant of healthy marrow. And if my marrow is the most like hers, I'm going to let her have it, no matter how much it hurts. In a way, I almost hope I *am* the one who matches best. If I am, I just hope my marrow will help her get better and won't attack her body. What a thing to think about.

I think about a lot of things lately though. Like animals used for research. I'm just all mixed up about it. I hate the thought of dogs like Casey being hurt, just so people can get better. But then I think about kids like Julie dying if there's no good way to test the drug that might save them.

But just because people think we're smarter and more important than animals, does that make it okay to use them for tests? What if some weird-looking aliens from space landed on Earth? What if they couldn't understand our language, and their civilization was so much more

179

advanced than ours that they thought we were a bunch of ignorant morons? What if they decided it would be okay to use *us* for experiments that might save aliens' lives just because they thought they were more important than we are? Would that make it okay?

Sorry to go on about it. I didn't mean for this letter to get so long.

I've been doing a lot of thinking about my future, too. I've decided that I'm going to go to college to be a medical researcher. But I'm not going to do tests on animals. I'm going to discover *new* ways to test drugs and cleaning stuff and makeup. Ways that don't need animals. Maybe by then we'll have made computers so smart they'll be able to do a lot of the testing. Maybe by then dogs like Casey won't have to die so that a person can live. (When I'm famous from developing all those tests, I *might* let you interview me for your television program.)

All for now. Write and let me know how you like junior high.

Your former partner in crime,
Scott

P.S. They're talking about banning pound seizure in my county. Maybe I've already started to make up for Casey.

Celebrating 40 Years of Cleary Kids!

CAMELOT presents
CLEARY FAVORITES!

- **HENRY HUGGINS**
  70912-0 ($3.99 US/$4.99 Can)

- **HENRY AND BEEZUS**
  70914-7 ($3.50 US/$4.25 Can)

- **HENRY AND THE
  CLUBHOUSE**
  70915-5 ($3.50 US/$4.25 Can)

- **ELLEN TEBBITS**
  70913-9 ($3.99 US/$4.99 Can)

- **HENRY AND RIBSY**
  70917-1 ($3.50 US/$4.25 Can)

- **BEEZUS AND RAMONA**
  70918-X ($3.50 US/$4.25 Can)

- **RAMONA AND HER FATHER**
  70916-3 ($3.99 US/$4.99 Can)

- **MITCH AND AMY**
  70925-2 ($3.50 US/$4.25 Can)

- **RUNAWAY RALPH**
  70953-8 ($3.50 US/$4.25 Can)

- **HENRY AND THE
  PAPER ROUTE**
  70921-X ($3.50 US/$4.25 Can)

- **RAMONA AND HER MOTHER**
  70952-X ($3.50 US/$4.25 Can)

- **OTIS SPOFFORD**
  70919-8 ($3.50 US/$4.25 Can)

- **THE MOUSE AND THE
  MOTORCYCLE**
  70924-4 ($3.99 US/$4.99 Can)

- **SOCKS**
  70926-0 ($3.50 US/$4.25 Can)

- **EMILY'S RUNAWAY
  IMAGINATION**
  70923-6 ($3.50 US/$4.25 Can)

- **MUGGIE MAGGIE**
  71087-0 ($3.99 US/$4.99 Can)

- **RAMONA THE PEST**
  70954-6 ($3.99 US/$4.99 Can)

From Out of the Shadows...
Stories Filled With Mystery and Suspense by
MARY DOWNING HAHN

THE TIME OF THE WITCH
71116-8/$3.50 US/$4.25 Can

It is the middle of the night and suddenly Laura is awake, trembling with fear. Just beneath her bedroom window, a strange-looking old woman is standing in the moonlight. A big black crow is perched on her shoulder and she is looking up—staring back at Laura.

STEPPING ON THE CRACKS
71900-2/$3.50 US/$4.25 Can

THE DEAD MAN IN INDIAN CREEK
71362-4/$3.50 US/$4.25 Can

THE DOLL IN THE GARDEN
70865-5/$3.50 US/$4.25 Can

FOLLOWING THE MYSTERY MAN
70677-6/$3.50 US/$4.25 Can

TALLAHASSEE HIGGINS
70500-1/$3.50 US/$4.25 Can

WAIT TILL HELEN COMES
70442-0/$3.50 US/$4.25 Can

Join in the Wild and Crazy Adventures with Some Trouble-Making Plants

by Nancy McArthur

THE PLANT THAT ATE DIRTY SOCKS

75493-2/$2.95 US/$3.50 Can

Michael's room was always a disaster area, strewn with all kinds of litter—heaps of paper and dirty socks everywhere. But that was before the appearance of the most amazing plants ever! Suddenly Michael's junk heap disappeared, eaten by two giant plants that gobbled up socks faster than anyone could supply them.

And Don't Miss

THE RETURN OF THE PLANT THAT ATE DIRTY SOCKS

75873-3/$2.95 US/$3.50 Can

It's vacation time and the sock eaters are going along with Michael and his family to Florida.

THE ESCAPE OF THE PLANT THAT ATE DIRTY SOCKS

76756-2/$3.50 US/$4.25 Can

Now that the sock-eating plants have learned to move themselves around, they're off on some wild adventures, with the whole family chasing after them.

Avon Camelot Presents
Award-Winning Author

THEODORE TAYLOR

THE CAY 00142-X/$3.50 US/$4.25 Can

After being blinded in a fatal shipwreck, Phillip was rescued from the shark-infested waters by the kindly old black man who had worked on deck. Cast up on a remote island, together they began an amazing adventure.

THE TROUBLE WITH TUCK

62711-6/$3.50 US/$4.25 Can

Twice Helen's dog Tuck had saved her life. And when she discovered he was going blind, she fought to become his eyes—now it was her turn to save *his* life.

TUCK TRIUMPHANT 71323-3/$3.50 US/$4.25 Can

At last...the miracle dog returns in the heartwarming sequel to *The Trouble with Tuck*.